"I want to be with you, Jody. And not just as a friend."

"B-but I..." God. She was sputtering. And why did she suddenly feel light as a breath of air, as if she was floating on moonbeams? "You want to be with me? But you don't do that. You've made that very clear."

"You're right. I didn't do that. Until now. But things have changed."

"Because of Marybeth, you mean?"

"Yeah, because of Marybeth. And because of you, too. Because of the way you are. Strong and honest and smart and so pretty. Because we've got something going on, you and me. Something good. I'm through pretending that we're friends and nothing more. Are you telling me I'm the only one who feels that way?"

"I just..." Her pulse raced and her cheeks felt too hot. She'd promised herself that nothing like this would happen, that she wouldn't get her hopes up.

She needed to be careful. She could end up with her heart in pieces all over again.

* * *

THE BRAVOS OF JUSTICE CREEK:
Where bold hearts collide under western skies

Dear Reader,

Jody Bravo is going to be the best single mom ever. The baby's due in six weeks and Jody's totally ready for the blessed event. She's fully self-supporting, with a successful flower shop and money in the bank. She has a big, close-knit family of Bravos to give her and her baby girl all the love and support they could ever need.

What she *doesn't* need is Sheriff Seth Yancy's help. The big, stern lawman may be her baby's uncle, but there's just something about him that gets under her skin.

Seth Yancy lives to serve the citizens of tiny Broomtail county. There's not much else left for him. Seven years ago, he lost what mattered most. And since then, the hits just keep on coming. But when someone finally tells him that Jody's unborn baby is his lost brother's little girl, Seth is bound and determined to do what he can for Nick's coming child. He's going to be there for Jody and the baby, whether Jody wants him around or not....

Jody and Seth are two wounded souls with a lot more in common than either of them realizes. They need each other. And Jody's baby needs them both.

And a story like theirs is why I love writing romance. Jody and Seth have a lot of work to do to make a life as full of love and happiness as they both deserve. I hope you get as caught up in their story as I did and that the ending leaves you satisfied—and smiling, too.

All my best,

Christine Rimmer

The Lawman's Convenient Bride

Christine Rimmer

Recycling programs
for this product may
not exist in your area.

ISBN-13: 978-0-373-62344-0

The Lawman's Convenient Bride

Copyright © 2017 by Christine Rimmer

Printed in U.S.A.

Christine Rimmer came to her profession the long way around. She tried everything from acting to teaching to telephone sales. Now she's finally found work that suits her perfectly. She insists she never had a problem keeping a job—she was merely gaining "life experience" for her future as a novelist. Christine lives with her family in Oregon. Visit her at christinerimmer.com.

Books by Christine Rimmer

Harlequin Special Edition

The Bravos of Justice Creek

A Bravo for Christmas
Ms. Bravo and the Boss
James Bravo's Shotgun Bride
Carter Bravo's Christmas Bride
The Good Girl's Second Chance
Not Quite Married

The Bravo Royales

A Bravo Christmas Wedding
The Earl's Pregnant Bride
The Prince's Cinderella Bride
Holiday Royale
How to Marry a Princess
Her Highness and the Bodyguard
The Rancher's Christmas Princess

Bravo Family Ties

A Bravo Homecoming
Marriage, Bravo Style!
Donovan's Child
Expecting the Boss's Baby

Visit the Author Profile page
at Harlequin.com for more titles.

For every brave soul who dares to love again.

Chapter One

Sheriff Seth Yancy worked hard for his community. He lived to serve the citizens of tiny Broomtail County, Colorado, and he would do just about anything for his constituents.

But a bachelor auction?

No way would he agree to be a prize in one of those. Being raffled off to the highest bidder was beneath his dignity. Plus, he would have to go out with the winner. Seth hadn't gone out with anyone in almost four years. And way back when he did go out, it hadn't been with a woman from town—or anywhere in Broomtail County, for that matter.

He was single and planned to stay that way. Dating someone who lived in his community, well, that could get messy. Seth didn't do messy. As sheriff, he tried to set a good example in all aspects of his personal life.

And that meant that when the president of the library association asked him to be a prize in her upcoming bachelor auction, Seth went right to work gently and regretfully turning her down.

He sat back in his new leather desk chair in his brand-new office in the recently opened Broomtail County Justice Center on the outer edge of the small town of Justice Creek and said, "The last Saturday in May? I'm sorry, Mrs. Carruthers. That's a bad day for me." It wasn't really a lie, he reasoned. Because if he said yes to the woman in the guest chair across from him, it *would* be a bad day.

"Call me Caroline." She crossed her slim legs and folded her hands on her knee.

"Sure, Caroline. What time did you say the auction was?"

"We're planning an all-day event in the park. But you would only need to be there between, say, two and four."

"Two and four," he repeated, stalling a little, as though he really did want to help her out. And he did. Just not for this.

Caroline beamed at him from behind her cat's-eye glasses. "So then. We can count on you as one of our bachelors. I'm so pleased."

"Hmm. Hold on, now. I'll have to check." He clicked the mouse on his desktop and made a show of frowning at the screen. "I'm sorry, but between two and four is impossible." It was an outright lie this time. And Seth did not approve of lying. But to get out of being raffled off like a prize bull, he would sink pretty low. "I just can't make it."

Caroline's sweet smile never wavered, though her eyes were a flinty, determined shade of gray. "Sheriff, I can't tell you how much it would mean to us if you could find a way to rearrange your schedule and say yes."

He cleared his throat, the sound downright officious even to his own ears. "I'm sorry. Really."

She adjusted her glasses, causing the beaded neck strap to twinkle aggressively. "Did I mention yet that the auction will help finance the library's new media center?"

"Yes, you did, and I—"

"It's a great cause. An important project. Children who don't have access to the internet need a chance to become familiar with the life tools others take for granted. And how many of our seniors wish they could broaden their horizons and move into the digital age? The center is so much more than just a bonus for our community. It's an out-and-out necessity."

"Yes, I understand that. But I really can't—"

"And it will take so little of your time, Sheriff. A couple of hours in Library Park the day of the auction and then one date with the lucky lady who bids the most for you. We've gotten Silver Star Limousine from Denver to donate a limo for your date. The winning ladies will each get a spa day at Sweet Harmony Day Spa. You'll be expected to pay for the date, of course, and I know you and the happy girl who wins you will choose something memorable and fun to do together."

"I understand, but as I keep trying to tell you, Caroline, I really can't."

"Oh, yes, you can." She blasted that smile at him, brighter than ever. "We all do admire the important work you do here. We're grateful for your service to this community."

"Well, thank you. I—"

"Of all the eligible bachelors in our county, I believe you are the most respected." Eligible? Seth might be single, but he was far from eligible. To be eligible, a man had to be willing to get involved in a relationship, and he wasn't. Caroline's gray eyes seemed to bore right through him. "Respected and so greatly admired. Word does get around. I've heard about your fan club..."

His fan club. He supposed that didn't sound so bad. At least she hadn't called them badge bunnies, which a lot of civilians considered cool police slang. Seth found the term sexist and objectifying—and, yes, he knew all about sexism. It was part of his job to know about it and to squelch it whenever it reared its ugly head. He didn't approve of terms that objectified anyone. And as for his "fan club," there weren't that many of them. But they were certainly enthusiastic, always dropping by to see him with baked goods and big smiles. Seth skirted a fine line with the women in question. He tried to be polite and appreciative while never letting any of them get too close.

If he gave in and said yes to the auction, one of them would probably "win" him. How awkward would that be?

He didn't even want to think about it.

And Caroline was still talking. "A tweak of your calendar, a few hours in the park and a date with a generous, community-conscious woman. Just one date. For the needy children who can so easily be left behind, for the seniors with ever-narrowing horizons."

He willed Garth Meany, the dispatcher, whose narrow back he could see through his inner-office window, to get a call—nothing too serious, a drunk and disorderly or someone creating a public nuisance. No one should get hurt. All Seth wanted was a chance to "notice" Garth on that call. He could bounce to his feet, mumble something about a "390" or a "507" that required his immediate attention—and hustle Caroline right out the door.

Unfortunately, it was a Tuesday afternoon in April, and the citizens of Broomtail County were apparently sober and behaving themselves. "Caroline, I'm so sorry, but I have another appointment in—"

"Just say the magic word, and I'll get out of your hair."

"But I—"

"Please." Now her eyes were huge and mournful behind the slanted, glittery frames. "Sheriff. We need you."

He opened his mouth to say no again. But Caroline looked so sad for all those disadvantaged children with no access to the internet, all those shut-in seniors who didn't even know how to send an email. He really did hate lying. And did she have to keep using that word, *need*?

Seth Yancy was a bitter man in many ways. His life hadn't turned out the way he'd once hoped it might. And the last few months, since the sudden death of his only brother, Nick, had been nothing but grim for him. Nicky was a good guy, the best. And way too young to die. It just wasn't right, that he'd been taken.

Too many were taken. And always the ones who deserved long, full lives.

But even though he'd been feeling more down than usual lately, Seth still liked to believe he was a good public servant, that when the people of his county needed him, one way or another, he would come through.

Caroline regarded him steadily, waiting for his reply.

And by then, for Seth, there was only one answer to give. "All right. I'll rearrange my schedule."

An hour later, Caroline was long gone, off to corner some other poor schmuck and badger him into making a fool of himself on the bachelor auction block. Seth was still in his office reviewing last month's budget overages, with the jail's operations report still to get through.

But enough. He was done for the day.

The budget and the reports could wait until tomorrow. After being bested by that Carruthers woman, he needed a fat, juicy steak and a twice-baked potato, and he knew where to get them.

The Sylvan Inn sat in a small wooded glen a few miles outside of town. At four thirty in the afternoon on a weekday, the parking lot had one row of cars in it—the row closest to the front entrance. Seth pulled in at the end of that row.

Inside, the hostess led him straight to a deuce by a window that looked out on a shaded patio. Perfect. He felt the cares of the day melting away.

Caroline Carruthers?

Never heard of her.

His waitress, Monique Hightower, appeared. Seth had known Monique for a good twenty years, at least. They'd attended Justice Creek High about the same time, with him graduating a couple of years ahead of her. She'd been working here at the Inn for a decade, maybe more.

"Hey, Seth. You're earlier than usual for a weekday." Monique refilled the water glass he'd already emptied and set the bread basket in front of him. "Everything okay?" Monique was a good waitress, but she talked too much. And she had a rep for being overly interested in other people's business.

He replied, "Everything is just fine, thanks," in a tone that discouraged further conversation. "I'll have the house salad with blue cheese, a Porterhouse, bloody, and a fully loaded potato." A beer would really hit the spot, but he was still in uniform. "And bring me a nice, big Coke."

Monique jotted down his order. "Be right back with your drink and that salad." She trotted off, blond corkscrew curls bouncing in her high ponytail.

She was as good as her word, too, bouncing right back over with a tall, fizzy Coca-Cola and a plateful of greens.

Seth buttered a hunk of hot bread and got down to the business of enjoying his meal. By the time the steak and potato arrived, he felt better about everything. The auction was almost six weeks away. He'd put it on his calendar, and he'd promised Caroline he would pose for a picture and work up a bio that would make the women of Justice Creek eager to bid on him. He wasn't looking forward to either activity, but as soon as they were accomplished, he could forget about the whole thing until he had to show up at the park the last Saturday in May.

"All done?" Monique stood at his elbow.

"Yeah. It was terrific, as always."

She took his plate. "Wait till you see the dessert cart. On the house for you, Seth."

"Thanks, Monique. Just the check."

And off she went, returning in no time with the bill. He gave her his credit card. Not three minutes after that, she set down the leather check folder on the white tablecloth. He put his card away and picked up the pen.

"So. Jody seems to be doing great, don't you think, all round and rosy?" It was Monique. For some reason, she'd remained standing right behind him.

He added the tip and scratched in his signature. "Jody?"

Monique leaned a little closer and spoke very softly. "Jody Bravo."

He remembered then. Jody Bravo. Pretty brunette. Daughter of Frank Bravo, deceased, and Frank's second wife, Willow Mooney Bravo. Willow Bravo was a piece of work. She'd carried on a decades-long affair with Frank while his rich first wife, Sondra, was still alive. Sondra had given Frank four children. Pretty much simultaneously, Willow had given him five. Including Jody, who owned a flower shop on Central.

Jody and Nick had been friends there for a while, at the end.

Monique said, "She's due next month, right?"

This was getting weird. "Due to…?"

"Have the baby, of course."

Evidently, Jody Bravo was pregnant. Given that she'd been a friend of Nicky's, he probably should have known that.

But why, exactly, did Monique Hightower think she ought to bring it up to him?

He dropped the pen on the open check folder. "Monique."

"Yeah?"

"Come on around here where I can see you."

She sidled into his line of sight looking uncomfortable now, giving him big eyes and a sweet never-mind of a smile. "So. Can I get you anything else?"

He hit her with his lawman's stare, dead-on with zero humor. "You went this far. Better finish it, whatever it is."

"Ahem." She slid a glance toward the kitchen, scoping out the location of her boss, no doubt. "I...thought you knew, that's all."

"Knew what?"

"Well, I mean that the baby Jody's having..." The sentence wandered off into nowhere.

"Go on."

"Well, Seth. It's, um, Nick's baby."

Nick's baby.

Seth heard a strange roaring in his ears, as though the ocean were right outside the window, giant waves beating on that pretty shaded patio. "Did you just say that Jody Bravo is having Nick's baby?"

Monique's curly knot of hair bobbed frantically with her nod. She leaned close and whispered, "I can't believe you haven't heard. I mean, I know he was your stepbrother, but you two were closer than most blood-related brothers. And it's not as if Jody's been keeping it a secret. Everybody knows that baby is Nick's, that it's a girl, due at the end of May."

The roaring of the invisible ocean got louder.

...it's a girl. Everybody knows...

Everybody but *him.*

Come to think of it, Nicky'd had a crush on that Bravo woman, hadn't he?

That was back in the late summer and fall, not long before Nick died. Nick had told Seth he had a thing for

Jody, but that Jody didn't feel the same, so they were "just friends."

Just friends. That had pissed Seth off. He'd wondered if that Bravo woman was leading his little brother on. After all, she had to be, what, eight or nine years older than Nick?

And Nicky had always been too easy, too tender and open, his big heart just begging for someone to break it. Maybe Jody Bravo had some idea that Nick wasn't good enough for her because he was a simple guy, happy to work the family ranch for a living, a guy who hadn't been to some fancy college.

If so, she was a fool. There was no man better than Nick.

And wait a minute. She came to the funeral, didn't she? Walked right up and shook Seth's hand, said how sorry she was.

But she didn't say a single word about any baby.

"Oh, look," Monique piped up nervously. "One of my other customers needs more coffee. Good to see you, Seth. Have a great day…" She was already bouncing away.

Seth let her go. He needed more information, but he knew better than to seek it from Monique. The invisible ocean still roaring inside his head, he rose, pushed his chair back under the table and headed for the door.

Once back in his cruiser, he started the engine and got out of there, turning back onto the highway going east, away from town. For a while, he just drove, tuning out the chatter on the scanner, willing his blood to stop thundering through his veins.

Had he planned to go home? Kind of. But he didn't. He blew right by the turnoff to the Bar-Y.

Maybe it wasn't even true. Monique was hardly a reliable source, after all; she could so easily be wrong about everything, or even lying.

But what if it *was* true?

Was that Bravo woman ever planning to tell him?

Halfway to I-25, at the small town of Lyons, he did turn the cruiser around. He went back the way he'd come. But he didn't take the turnoff to the Bar-Y then, either. He drove on past it and straight into town, where he found a parking place right on Central a few doors down from Jody Bravo's flower shop.

At twenty past six, he stood between the tubs of bright flowers and thick greenery that flanked the shop's glass door. His pulse thundering louder than ever, he went in. A little bell tinkled overhead, and Jody Bravo, behind the counter across the room, glanced his way.

Even with the counter masking her body from the waist down, he could see she was pregnant. And pretty far along, too. That belly looked ready to pop.

He let his gaze track upward to her face. Did she pale at the sight of him? He couldn't be sure. But she definitely looked wary, her soft mouth drawn tight, a certain watchfulness in her eyes.

"Sheriff," she said coolly. "I'll be right with you." And she turned a friendly smile to the older man she was waiting on. "Roses and lilies." She passed him a paper-wrapped cone full of flowers. "Excellent choice. I know she'll love them…"

Seth hovered near the door, not sure what to do with himself. Another customer came in, and he moved to the side to clear the entrance. And then he just stood there, surrounded by greenery, breathing that moist, sweet smell created by so many flowers and growing things pressing in close.

"Seth?" asked the Bravo woman as the second customer went out the door.

He realized he was staring blankly at a hanging basket full of cascading purple flowers. "Right here," he answered, though she was standing directly behind him and no doubt looking straight at him. He turned around and met those wary eyes. "We need to talk."

Resigned. She looked resigned. His certainty increased that Monique had not lied; that giant belly cradled his brother's child.

Nicky's baby. He didn't know what he felt. Joy, maybe. And something else, something angry and ready for a fight.

She said, "It's time to close. I need to bring in the stock from out in front and deal with the register."

"I'll help."

"No, it's fine. I can—"

"I said, I'll help." It came out as a growl.

She stiffened, but then she answered calmly, "Well. All right, then. If you'll bring in the flowers." She gestured at a section of bare floor space not far from the door. "Just put them there for now."

"For now?"

"I'll take them to the cooler in back later."

"As long as I'm bringing them in, I can take them where you want them to go." He put out a hand toward the glass-doored refrigerator full of fancy arrangements that took up much of one wall. "You want them in there?"

She bit her lip like she was about to argue with him. But then she said, "No, there's a walk-in cooler in back."

She pointed at the café doors near the check-out counter. "Through there."

"All right, then. I'll bring everything in."

They got to it. She turned off the Open sign and closed out the register while he carried in the tubs of flowers, trekking them through the inner door to the other fridge. Once all the tubs were in, she locked the shop door. There was an ironwork gate between her shop and the one next door, but it was shut, the shop on the other side dark and quiet.

She must have seen him glance that way. "My half sister Elise owns Bravo Catering and Bakery through there. She closed at six."

And so they were alone, with no chance of interruption.

He got to the point. "I heard a rumor that you're having my brother's baby."

He didn't know what he'd expected. Denial? Nervousness? An apology for holding out on him?

But all he got from her was the barest hint of a shrug, followed by a quietly spoken confirmation. "Yes. Nick was my baby's father."

The soft words struck him like blows. All at once, his ears were burning. His stomach clenched, and he really wished he hadn't eaten so much steak.

Sucking in a long breath through his nose, he accused, "You were at the funeral."

"Yes."

"You stepped right up to me. You shook my hand. You had to know there was a baby then."

"Yes, I did."

"But you said nothing." He gave her a look meant to make her knees shake and waited for her to explain herself. When she only regarded him steadily, he demanded, "What is the matter with you? Why am I the last to know? My brother has been dead for almost six months, and until Monique Hightower shared the news today, I had no idea there was a baby involved."

That seemed to get through to her. Scowling now, she whipped up a hand, palm flat in his face. "Don't you get on me, Sheriff. I thought you knew—and didn't care."

Didn't care? That knocked him back. He took a moment to gather his composure. And then he said, deadly calm, "You thought wrong. Did Nick even know?"

Slowly, she lowered her hand to her side. Her diamond-shaped face was all eyes at that moment, eyes of a blue so deep they looked black. Those eyes stared right through him. "He knew."

Seth couldn't help but scoff when she said that. "Oh, no. Uh-uh."

"Why even ask if you're not willing to accept my answer?"

"I guess I had some crazy idea you might tell me the truth."

"That *is* the truth."

"How long did he know?"

"I told him a few days after I found out myself. That was about six weeks before he died."

"I don't believe you."

Twin spots of color flamed high on her cheeks. "Keep calling me a liar, and I'm just going to have to ask you to leave."

Was he out of line? Probably. A little. But she should have told him that his dead brother had fathered a child. And that she'd told Nicky? He couldn't see it. "Nick was a stand-up guy. If he'd known there was a baby, he would have wanted to marry you. That was who he was, a simple man with a big heart and high standards, a man whose own natural father deserted him *and* his mother. Nick wouldn't do that. If he knew about that baby, you'd have a ring on your finger—and there is no way that he would have..." His throat locked up. He swallowed hard to loosen it and then tried again. "If Nick knew he was going to be a father, he would've told *me*."

Chapter Two

Jody Bravo stared at the shiny badge pinned to the starched khaki dress shirt right above Seth Yancy's heart and tried to decide what to say next.

Unlike Nick, who'd been lean and wiry, of medium height, Seth was a tall man, imposing, built broad and tough. Not as handsome as Nick, but a good-looking man if you liked them strong-jawed and dripping testosterone. He was one of those guys who looked like a cop in or out of his uniform, as if he'd been born to protect and serve and would do so whether you wanted him to or not. He wore his brown hair clipped short and his posture was ramrod-straight.

His anger with her? It came off him in waves.

Yes, she should have told him about the baby earlier. She supposed. In hindsight. But she found him so... forbidding. At the funeral, when she'd offered her condolences, he'd narrowed his eyes at her and muttered a grudging *thank you*. She'd read his attitude loud and clear; he couldn't wait for her to move on. So, yeah, she'd kept putting off telling him, kept asking herself why it even mattered if the step-uncle knew about Nick's baby or not? At the same time, she'd had some vague plan to go see him, have a little talk with him, eventually, when the moment felt right.

But the moment never felt right. Also, she really had wondered if he knew about the baby already and simply didn't care. So, yeah, she'd been struggling with a powerful desire never to have to deal with the guy in any way, shape or form.

But right now she just felt sorry for him. So what if he was acting like a first-class douche canoe with his judgmental attitude and insensitive accusations?

The man missed his baby brother. And he was hurt that Nick hadn't confided in him.

As for the marriage question, she didn't even want to get into that with him. But still. He was here and clearly he cared. She gave him the truth. "Nick did ask me to marry him. I turned him down."

"Why?"

She did know what he meant by the curtly uttered question, but she was feeling just snarky enough to ask for clarification anyway. "Why did he ask me, you mean?"

"Why did you turn him down?" He barked that one at her.

Stay calm, she reminded herself. "Nick was a wonderful guy. He deserved a woman who loved him with all of her heart."

His lip curled in a sneer. "And you didn't."

"You should stop talking," she said with excruciating sweetness. "Because I have to tell you, Seth. Every time you open your mouth, you give me a new reason *not* to be nice to you. I'm sorry Nick didn't tell you. But I was only three months pregnant when he died. I'm sure he thought he had plenty of time."

"Plenty of time. My God. Plenty of…" Seth shook his head. His upper lip was sweating.

Again, her exasperation with him faded.

Nick had told her all about the big brother he admired so much. He'd said Seth was the kind of man you wanted at your back in a tough situation, always cool and even-tempered, a man who kept command of himself and his emotions no matter how bad things got.

But right now, Seth Yancy was far from cool. He stared at a point somewhere beyond her left shoulder. It seemed to her he hovered on the brink of losing it completely.

Jody stepped forward and wrapped her fingers around his rock-hard forearm. "Seth."

He flinched and blinked down at her hand. "What?"

"It's okay."

"I don't…"

"Shh. Come on." She pulled him to a bentwood chair by the window, an old one she'd decorated by painting it with twining vines and little flowers. "Sit right here. Let me get you some water…" She gently pushed him down.

He resisted. "No. No, I'm all right."

"Humor me?" she coaxed.

Slowly, he sank into the chair. She let go of his arm— and he grabbed her hand. "Look. Honestly. I don't know what my problem is. I shouldn't have been so hard on you…"

"It's okay," she soothed.

"I apologize. I didn't know you were having Nicky's baby. I really didn't know."

"It's okay…"

He blinked and frowned up at her. "You keep saying that."

"Because I have this feeling that you're not hearing me."

He kept hold of her fingers with one hand and scrubbed the other one down his face. "I heard you."

Gently, she pulled free of his grip. "Stay here. I'll be right back."

Seth did what she asked of him. He sat there in that spindly chair until she returned with a bottled water. "Here you go. Drink." She pressed it into his hand.

He stared up at her, at her worried eyes and her serious mouth. "I'm not usually such a jackass."

Her mouth twitched in the beginnings of a smile she didn't quite let happen. "I really do understand. I'm sure it's a shock."

"I…"

She tapped the sweating water bottle. "It's nice and cold. Drink."

It wasn't a bad suggestion, especially given that his mouth felt like he'd just swallowed a bucket of sand. So he unscrewed the lid and put the bottle to his lips. He drank it down in one go.

"Better?" she asked.

"Yeah. Thanks—and I am sorry. I don't know what got into me."

"You're forgiven." She spoke softly. Her eyes were kind now.

He had a thousand questions to ask her. He hardly knew where to start. But what he did know was that he *would* be a part of Nick's baby's life. "I want to help. Any way I can."

"Well, thank you…" The words were right. Her expression wasn't. She bit the corner of her lip and fell back a step.

He wanted to grab her arm and pull her in close again. "What's wrong with my wanting to help?"

"Nothing. Nothing at all. It's very kind of you, and I appreciate the offer. Right now, though, there's nothing to help me with. I'm all set."

"Set? How's that?"

"Honestly, there's nothing more to do at this point. I've got everything handled. I have excellent insurance and I'm getting great prenatal care. I'm watching my diet, taking my vitamins. The baby and I are both in good health. The baby's room is ready. My sisters are all three helping out, planning to be with me through labor and delivery. I have full-time backup here at the store for those first weeks after the birth. My due date is a month and a half away, and I'm all ready to go."

"Well, great," he replied, though to him it was anything but. He needed to help her, and how could he do that if she had everything under control?

She added too brightly, "But I promise I'll be in touch as soon as she's born."

"It's a she?" he parroted blankly, remembering that Monique had said the baby would be a girl.

"Yes." Jody did manage a smile then. "Her name is Marybeth."

Marybeth. Nicky's little girl will be named Marybeth. "I still want to help."

"And you can."

"Tell me what to do."

A nervous laugh escaped her. "As I said, I can't think of anything right now, but you never know…" The way she was looking at him? Not good. Like she wished he would leave, and the sooner the better.

And he couldn't blame her for wanting him gone. He'd jumped down her throat, done a first-class imitation of an overbearing ass, when he should have been gentle and coaxing and kind.

He really ought to go. He should retreat and regroup—and do a better job of acting like a civilized human being the next time he talked to her.

So all right. Next time would be better. He bent to set the water bottle on the floor, lifted the flap on his right breast pocket and pulled out one of the business cards the county provided for him. "Got a pen?"

"Uh. Sure." She zipped over to the counter with the register on it and came back with a Bic.

He took it and jotted his private numbers on the back of the card. "Call me at the justice center anytime, for anything. And you can reach my cell and the phone at the ranch with the numbers on the back."

"I… Great. Thanks." She accepted the card and the return of her pen and looked down at him expectantly, waiting for him to get up and get out.

And he would. Soon. But first there were things he had to tell her, stuff she needed to know. "After we lost Nicky, I moved to the ranch."

"Ah. That's right. You used to live in…?"

"Prideville." The former county seat was a forty-mile drive from Justice Creek. "With the justice center here now, I wanted to be nearby anyway. And my dad retired to Florida a few years back. We've got a great couple, Mae and Roman Califano, out at the Bar-Y. They're good people. And they can run the place with their hands tied behind their backs. But I think it's important to have someone in the family living there."

"Yes. Yes, I can see that."

"You know how to get to the Bar-Y, right? You've been there, haven't you?"

"Yes. I have, a few times, actually—last fall, after Nick and I became friends. And I've met the Califanos, too. I liked them."

He tried not to stare at her belly. He had a yen to touch it, to see if the baby might give a little kick, provide him with tangible proof that Nicky's child lived.

But he knew he'd blown his chances for any belly-feeling today. "Just in case, I can jot down the address for you..."

"No. Really, I know how to get to the Bar-Y—I mean, if I need to get there." Her gaze shifted toward the door and then right back to him, as though she could hustle him out with the flick of a glance. He took another card from his pocket and held it out to her.

He watched a dimple tucking itself in at the corner of her mouth. "Seth." She held up the first card. "I already have one."

"Jody, I would really appreciate having your numbers, too." He said it hopefully, pouring on the sincerity, though as sheriff, he would have no trouble getting his hands on just about anything he needed to know about her. But it was better if she volunteered her contact information. That way when he called, it would be because she'd given him tacit permission to do so.

"Oh. Well, sure." She accepted the card, scribbled on the back of it and returned it to him.

"Great." He stuck the card back in his pocket. And then, reluctantly, he stood.

She flew to the door, turned the lock and pulled it open. "Thanks, Seth. I'm…glad you came by."

No, she wasn't. But it was nice of her to say so. "Call me. I mean it. Anytime."

"Yes. All right. I will."

He didn't believe her. But that was okay. If she didn't get in touch with him, he would be contacting her.

He was helping out whether she wanted him to or not.

"So will you call him?" Elise asked the next morning at the bakery. Three or four days a week, they shared breakfast at a small table tucked away in a corner. Bravo Catering and Bakery was already open. Jody would open Bloom in half an hour.

Jody leaned toward her sister across the table. "I have zero reason to call that man." She kept her voice low in order not to share her private business with every customer in the place.

Elise fiddled with her ginormous engagement diamond. She did that a lot, usually while smiling dreamily. She and Jed Walsh, the famous thriller writer, were getting married at the end of June. And actually, she was looking more thoughtful than dreamy right at the moment. "He's the baby's uncle, right? And he really wants to help. You said so yourself."

"There's nothing to help with. I'm so completely on top of this whole situation. You guys threw me three showers. There's nothing left to buy. The baby could come tomorrow. I'm ready to go. I mean, I have three birth coaches, present company included."

Elise gave a little snort. "You are so efficient I can't stand it. I get it. You've got this. It's all under control."

"As a matter of fact, it is. And I do."

"Kids do need family, though."

"Handled. We're Bravos. There are too many of us to count."

"Seth Yancy is your baby's family, too—and I can't believe I even have to remind you of that."

Jody stared into her steaming cup of rooibos tea. "Okay, Leesie. I get it. And I know you're right." She took a thoughtful sip. "I'll…reach out to him."

"You do realize you shudder when you say that?"

"I find him intimidating, okay? And the way he looks at me." She couldn't suppress another shiver. "Like I need a good talking-to, you know? Like I wasn't brought up properly and my moral compass is all out of whack."

Loyal to the core, Elise jumped right to Jody's defense. "Well, that's just rude. Maybe I should have a word with him."

Jody snorted a laugh. "Don't you dare—and really, he's not *that* bad. He was upset that I hadn't told him about the baby. And he was curt with me at Nick's funeral, but that's understandable. Nobody's at their best after losing a brother out of nowhere in a tractor accident."

"So. You'll give him a chance, then?"

"Yeah. Yeah, I will." But not until later. She had it all together this time around. She didn't need Seth Yancy's help.

True, he had a right to know his niece. And he would. After Marybeth was born, she would give him a call.

Elise said, "A week from Saturday Jed has to fly to New York for some publicity thing. He wants me to go."

"Can you afford to be away? Don't we have two parties that weekend?" Jody used the word *we* loosely. Her part would be minimal. Bloom would provide floral centerpieces for both events.

"They're just small dinner parties. Danielle can run them." Danielle was Elise's second in command at Bravo Catering.

"So go."

"I don't know. I want to be here for you, in case you need me."

Jody groaned. "Oh, please. I'm in perfect health. The baby is doing great, and I'm not due till the end of May. And if anything happened—which it won't—Nellie and Clara are a phone call away." Nell Bravo and Clara Ames were their other two sisters.

Elise fiddled with her ring some more. "I would be gone for four days, Saturday through Tuesday."

"Not a problem."

"It seems like a long time."

"Elise. Stop worrying."

"I'm trying."

"I've had no cramping, no spotting, not a single sign that the baby might be early."

"And besides, first babies usually come late, right?"

"Right." Jody tried not to look guilty.

Okay, so she had a few secrets. And somehow, she'd never gotten around to sharing them with her sisters, or anyone else in the family, for that matter—well, except for her mother. Somehow, Willow Bravo, of all people, had figured it out and shown up on her doorstep when Jody was six months along. As far as Jody knew, though, her mother had never told another soul.

And, no, Jody wasn't ashamed that she'd given her first baby up for adoption. All things considered, her choice had been the right one. And no one was going to judge her, anyway. She really ought to stop lying by omission and tell Elise and the rest of them the real reason she'd suddenly decided to spend several months in Sacramento at the age of eighteen.

But come on. It was thirteen years ago, which definitely put it into the category of old news. And she just didn't feel up to going into it now.

Kind of like she didn't feel up to reaching out to Seth Yancy…

On second thought, maybe there had been a little damage to her moral compass, after all.

"Jody?" Elise was watching her through suddenly worried eyes. "You okay?"

Jody pulled it together. "I am just fine. And *you're* going to New York with Jed."

The following Tuesday, Jody stood at the design station at Bloom. She was shaving the corners off a cube of floral foam when in walked the sheriff. Again.

Jody put down her knife with care. "Hello, Seth."

He took off his aviator sunglasses and his County Mounty hat and came right for her. "You never called." He set the hat on the counter and the glasses beside it.

Careful not to let anything spill on his hat, she brushed the shaved bits of foam from her hands. "There was no reason to call you. Everything is fine."

"You're sure?" He regarded her solemnly, with bleak concentration, as though if he stared hard enough, he could see inside her head and discover all the ways she wasn't taking proper care of herself.

Jody had a burning need to let out a long, exasperated sigh. Somehow, she quelled that. "I'm sure."

"Should you be on your feet so much?"

She was suddenly glad for the deep counter between them. He couldn't look down and see her slightly swollen ankles—which were nothing out of the ordinary for a woman in her third trimester. "Honestly. I'm taking excellent care of myself."

He sent a suspicious glance around the shop. "Those tubs of flowers outside are heavy. You should have help carrying them in at night."

She had a good answer for that one. "And I do have help. Plenty of it."

"How so?"

What? He had to have specifics as to her employees and the hours they worked? Fine. She would give him specifics. "I hired an extra assistant. I already have one who comes in to work with me on Saturday, runs the shop on Sunday by herself and picks up the slack whenever I need her. The new one comes in at two and stays through closing, Monday through Friday. And when the baby's born, she'll be here full-time for as long as I need her, and my original assistant will be working more, too." Was that enough information to end this interrogation?

Apparently not. "You were here on your own a week ago when we talked." It came out as an accusation with *How could you be so irresponsible?* implied at the end of it.

No way I have to explain myself to you. But then she went ahead and did it anyway. "The new girl called in sick that day. But she hasn't missed a day since. And if she can't make it, and the other clerk is busy, I have more people I can call."

"What about when you open up in the morning?"

"What about it?"

"Who carries all those tubs of flowers outside then?"

Seriously. Was this in any way his business? No. But if she told him to butt out, he might just decide to stick around and explain in detail all the reasons he had a right to cross-examine her. And what she really wanted was for him to go away. "For weeks now, my sister Elise or one of her clerks has been helping me open up every morning that I'm here on my own."

"I'd be happy to come by and pitch in."

"I… Thank you. I'll remember that."

"You still have my card with my numbers?"

Where had she put that? "I do. Yes. Of course."

"Jody." He gave her that laser-eyed stare again. "Did you lose my card?"

"No. Of course not."

"Show it to me."

She stood very still and reminded herself sternly that she was not going to start yelling at him. "I don't have it handy. Sorry."

The sheriff was not pleased. He pulled out a cell phone and punched some numbers into it. Her cell, in the pocket of her bib apron, blooped. "I've sent you my numbers. Again."

"Thanks." She knew she didn't sound the least appreciative, and by then, she didn't even care.

He took another of his cards from his breast pocket, grabbed a pen from the jar on the corner of the counter and wrote down all his private numbers all over again.

"Just to make sure you don't lose them this time." He held it out to her.

She didn't take it. "Seth, come on. You already put them in my phone."

"What if you lose your phone?"

"I won't." She folded her arms and rested them on her protruding stomach. "And anyway, I still have the first card you gave me. It's around. Somewhere." They glared at each other.

"I just want to help." He said it gently, but there was no mistaking the disapproval in his eyes.

And then the shop bell over the door jingled, saving her from saying something she shouldn't. Two well-dressed middle-aged women came in. "I have customers," she said with a blatantly unfriendly smile. "If you'll excuse me." She sidled out from behind the counter and made for the newcomers. "Hello, ladies. How may I help you?"

By the time she'd sold the women a mixed bouquet each, Seth had given up and left. She found the card he'd been trying to hand her on the design counter next to the partially shaved cube of foam. Shaking her head, she stuck it in her apron pocket.

And then she banished Seth Yancy from her thoughts.

Humming softly to herself, she went back to work arranging peonies, roses, green hydrangeas, maidenhair ferns and two gorgeous green-tipped purple Fiesole artichokes in a mercury glass compote bowl.

On Friday, Seth called her at home. He wanted to know how she was doing. She said she felt great.

He said, "If you need anything, you'll call me?"

"Absolutely," she replied and refused to think too deeply as to whether or not that was true.

A few minutes after she hung up, she got another call—this time on her cell. It was her sister Nell, who ran a construction business with their brother Garrett. Nellie wanted to fly to Phoenix that weekend for a home show. "Just checking in to be sure you're doing all right before I even think about deserting you."

"You're not deserting me. Nothing is happening here. Go."

"I might stay over until Tuesday or Wednesday. Visit with an...old friend."

"You know you sort of paused before the 'old friend' part, right?"

"What can I say? It's a business-with-pleasure kind of situation."

"Nellie."

"Um?"

"Have a fabulous time."

"I will—and you *would* tell me if there were any signs you're going into labor, right? Any spotting or weird cramping or if the baby had dropped?"

"Of course I would. My due date is four weeks out, and there's nothing to worry about."

Nellie started waffling. "You know, the more I think about it, four weeks isn't that far off. Anything could happen in the meantime."

"Nellie. Stop. There is nothing for you to worry about. And anyway, Clara's here if I need her."

"And also Elise," Nellie added helpfully.

Jody hesitated. She really didn't want Nell to talk herself out of the trip.

"Jo-Jo, you're too quiet."

So she confessed, "Elise is taking a quick trip to New York with Jed for some publicity event."

"You didn't tell me that Elise took off." Nellie said it in a chiding tone.

"She didn't. Yet. She's leaving tomorrow and will be back Tuesday and you'll be back Wednesday, and how many times do I have to tell you that I'm experiencing no signs of approaching labor, but if anything happens, I can call Clara. Or Rory." Rory McKellan was their cousin. "Or one of the guys if it comes down to it." They had five brothers and all of them lived in the area. Four of those brothers were either married or engaged to women Jody counted as friends. "There is no shortage of people I can call in an emergency."

Nell made a humming sound. "You really are sure about this?"

"How many times do I have to say it?"

Nell blew out an audible breath. "Sorry I got so freaky."

"Not complaining. I love that you care."

"I mean, you've had a textbook pregnancy, and you're healthy as a horse."

"Is this where I make a neighing sound?"

"Har-har. And it is your first baby and first babies—"

"Usually come late," Jody finished for her, wishing never to hear that particular phrase again.

"Love you, Jo-Jo."

"Love you, too. Call me when you get home."

"Will do."

She'd barely hung up when the phone blooped with a text. It was Seth.

You sure you don't need anything?

She actually chuckled as she texted back. Who are you and how did you get this number?

It wasn't easy, let me tell you. Call me. Anytime.

Absolutely. Will do.

The next day was Saturday. Nell flew to Phoenix and Elise and Jed took off for New York. Seth called that night. Just to check on her, he said. She told him yet again how well she was doing and he let her go.

Sunday, Lois Simonson, one of her two employees, ran the store all day. Jody stayed home and took it easy. She sat around in her pj's with her feet up and binge-watched the second season of *Outlander*—really, where was her own Jamie Fraser? She'd been waiting for him for most of her life. A couple of times she'd dared to hope she'd found what she was looking for.

Wrong on both counts.

And Nick? He'd been a sweetheart. But she'd known from the first that he wasn't the guy for her.

She put her hand on her giant belly and grinned to herself. She had Marybeth now. Her little girl would be enough for her. She would be a good mom and raise her child to know she could make anything she wanted of her life. And she would always have her sisters and her brothers and a network of in-laws and friends to count on and love.

Who needed a man?

Seth called that night, too. She grinned when she saw it was him. Was she kind of getting used to hearing his deep, careful voice?

Maybe. A little.

"What have you been doing?" he asked.

"Nothing. I have the day off, so I've been taking up space on the couch, watching TV."

"Good," he said. It was the first time she'd ever heard anything approaching approval in his voice when he talked to her. "And I know you're eating right. At least, that's what you tell me every time I call."

"Well, there was that carton of Ben and Jerry's Chunky Monkey and now it's gone. But otherwise, I had breakfast, lunch and dinner, and all three were comprised of heart-healthy, fiber-rich, nutritious ingredients. And you're kind of like an old mother hen, you know that?" There was a choked sort of sound from his end. "Seth Yancy, did you just almost laugh?"

"Me? Not a chance. Do you need anything?"

"Such as...?"

"Food. Supplies. Bottled water?"

"Are we preparing for the zombie apocalypse?"

"Just answer the question."

"No, Seth. As I keep telling you, I have everything I need, and if there's something I've forgotten, well, they have supermarkets now where I can pick up whatever I've run out of."

"You're being sarcastic."

"You noticed."

"And that reminds me. Should you even be driving?"

"Yes. I definitely should. And I do. Anything else?"

"Look. I'm trying really hard not to annoy you."

"I know that. And I thank you for it."

"I just want to—"

"—help. I know. And I appreciate it, Seth. But I've run out of ways to tell you that I am taking care of myself and there's nothing, really, to help me with."

He was so quiet she thought he'd hung up.

"Seth?"

"Right here. Okay, then. I'll check in tomorrow."

"Did I mention that the baby isn't due for weeks yet?"

"Yeah. Got that."

"So…are you planning to call every day?"

More silence. Finally, he asked, "Are you telling me not to?"

Yes! But somehow, she couldn't say that. Because it was so painfully obvious that he cared about his brother's unborn baby and he really did want to help. "No. It's okay." It came out sulky and grudging. "Let me try that again. I mean, thank you for, you know, being here. And I'll talk to you tomorrow, then."

"All right." Was that gravel-and-granite voice of his marginally softer? She couldn't be sure. "Sleep well, Jody."

She felt another smile curve her lips. "Good night, Seth."

Monday, he showed up at Bloom again just before closing time.

Jody was only too happy to introduce him to Marlie Grant, her second clerk and floral designer. Marlie, like Lois, had a talent with flowers and could be trusted not only to handle design and selling, but also to purchase stock from the wholesalers and flower farms nearby. Marlie took the last customer of the day, leaving Jody at the design station with Seth.

"I told you I had help," she said smugly as soon as Marlie was busy with old Mr. Watsgraff, who came in every Monday to buy a dozen white roses for his wife of forty-nine years.

"I'm staying to carry in the flowers." He made it sound like a threat.

"Fine. Help out. Be that way."

"You look tired."

She leaned toward him across the counter—as much as her giant stomach would allow, anyway. "Don't start in. Please."

Was that the beginnings of a grin tipping the corners of his bleak slash of a mouth? "Or you'll what?"

"I have an in with the sheriff's office is all I'm saying, so you'd better watch your step."

"Yes, ma'am." He said it quietly, and the sound sent a little shiver running down the backs of her knees.

She'd heard he had several feminine admirers in town, nice single women who often showed up at the justice center bringing cookies and wearing bright, hopeful smiles.

Until that moment, she'd never understood what they saw in him. Yeah, he was young to be sheriff. And hot and muscled up and manly and all that. But up till the last couple of check-in calls, she'd also found him overbearing and judgmental, which had pretty much made her immune to his fabled hotness.

But right now, when he almost smiled at her and then said *Yes, ma'am*, all teasing and low, well, she could see the appeal. A little bit. Maybe.

As soon as old Mr. Watsgraff went out the door with his cone of roses, Jody turned off the Open sign, and Marlie and Seth brought in the stock from outside.

He hung around until after Marlie left and then walked Jody out to her Tahoe in back.

"How about some dinner?" he asked, still holding the door open after helping her up behind the wheel.

She was actually tempted. But she was also uncomfortable with the idea. Would he ask her about Nick, want more details of their supposed romance, which had actually not been a romance at all? She wasn't ready to get into that with him and probably never would be.

"Thanks, Seth. But I just want to go home and put my feet up."

He gave a slight nod. "Well, that's understandable. I'll follow you, see that you get home safe."

"Seth." She looked at him steadily and then shook her head.

He gave it up. "Talk to you tomorrow."

"Good night."

He swung the door shut at last.

At home, she cooked a nice dinner of chicken breasts, steamed broccoli and rice, but when she sat down to eat, she just wasn't hungry. She felt at loose ends, somehow. Edgy, full of energy.

A little bit nervous.

She wandered aimlessly through her house, which she loved, a cozy traditional one-story, with a modern kitchen, a sunny great room and three bedrooms. Her father had made sure that each of his nine children were well provided for. Jody's trust fund had matured when she was twenty-one, and a year later, during the housing bust, she'd gotten an amazing deal on her place in a short sale. It was more house than she'd needed at the time, but she'd bought it anyway. Now it was worth three times what she'd paid for it, and with the baby coming, she was glad for the extra space.

In the baby's room, she lingered. She spent a half an hour admiring everything, touching the tiny onesies and the stacks of cotton blankets, hardly daring to believe that in a month, she would hold her baby in her arms. It was adorable, that room, if she did say so herself, with teal blue walls and bedding in coral and teal, cream and mint green. It had a mural of bright flowers and butterflies on one wall, and the whole effect was so pretty and inviting, all ready for Marybeth, even though she wouldn't be using it for a while. At first, she'd have a bassinet in Jody's room.

Eventually, she wandered out to the great room and tried to watch TV, but she couldn't concentrate.

She called Clara, who was down with the flu, of all things. Her husband, Dalton, had it, too, and so did their two-year-old, Kiera. Jody ordered her to get well, and Clara answered wryly that she was working on it.

After hanging up with Clara, she had the ridiculous desire to call Seth. But that would only encourage him, and that didn't seem right.

She went to bed at nine thirty and couldn't get comfortable, even with her body pillow to help support her belly and another pillow at her back. She was just sure she would never get to sleep.

But then the next thing she knew, she looked over at the bedside clock, and it was after two in the morning.

And something was…

She put her hands on her belly, felt the powerful, involuntary tightening, as though her body had a mind of its own.

"Dear, sweet God…"

With an animal growl, she threw back the covers and slithered to the floor, where she crouched like a crab on the bedside rug, groaning and huffing, fingers splayed over her rippling stomach as a second-stage contraction bore down like an extra pair of giant, cruel hands, pushing so hard she would have buckled under the pressure if she wasn't already on her knees.

She panted her way through it, and when it was over, she realized there was liquid dripping down her inner thighs. Her water had broken.

Her water had broken.

And Clara had the flu, Elise was in New York, and Nellie had gone to Phoenix.

But not to panic. Uh-uh. She'd done this before and she could do it again.

One hand still on her belly, she reached up and grabbed her phone off the nightstand. And then she just sat there, half expecting to wake up in her bed and discover that she really wasn't in active labor, after all; it was only a dream.

But then another one started.

Okay. No dream.

She used her phone to time that one as she squatted on the floor, moaning and grunting, the pain rising to a peak at thirty-two seconds, after which it faded back down. Once it was over, she estimated she had three to five minutes until the next one hit.

Time to find a ride to the hospital and then get in touch with her doctor—well, past time for both, actually.

But she refused to freak. Because there was nothing to be alarmed about. She was in labor, yes, but she had it under control. Her birth coaches might be unavailable, but at least there were plenty of people she could call. Even in the middle of the night, someone ought to be able to come pick her up and take her to Justice Creek General.

And if they weren't, well, there was always Uber. Or 911.

She brought up her cousin Rory's number and almost hit Call.

But then, for no comprehensible reason except that he kept insisting he really wanted to help, she scrolled down to Seth's cell number and called him instead.

Chapter Three

He answered on the first ring, sounding wide-awake—as though he'd been sitting up with his phone in his hand in the middle of the night, waiting for her to call. "Jody. What can I do?"

Her mind chose that moment to go blank. "I…need…"

"Anything. Yes." His voice was so calm, so even and strong. She felt she could reach right through the phone and grab on to him to steady herself. "What do you need?"

It was a simple question, and she had the answer ready. Except when she opened her mouth it was like pulling wide the floodgates on a full dam. "Elise and Nellie are out of town, and Clara's got the flu. I was going to call Rory, but then I thought of you and I…" He started to say something. But she didn't let him. She babbled right over him. "They all think it's my first and the first one always comes late, and I never corrected them, never *told* them. Because that's kind of how I am, you know? I keep too much to myself, I want to have it together and take care of business, and I end up pushing people away because I'm so self-sufficient. And now here I am on the bedroom floor, dripping all over the rug, without my birth coaches in the middle of the night. It's like I'm being punished by fate for lying to everyone about the first one, you know?"

"Jody."

"Um?"

"What do you mean, dripping?"

The note of alarm in his voice had her rushing to reassure him. "It's not that much. I exaggerated."

"You're not making sense."

"You're probably right."

"And, Jody, you said 'the first one.' The first what?"

"Baby," she blurted out and then slapped her hand over her big, fat mouth. Oh, God. She hadn't even told her sisters, and here she was, blathering it all out to Seth, who might want to help and all but still remained essentially a stranger to her.

"So," he tried again, clueless but still determined to stick with her and give her whatever she'd called him in the middle of the night to get. "Are you saying you feel guilty because—"

"Never mind. Doesn't matter. It's not why I called."

Dead silence. Then, "Okay. Let's go with that. Why did you call?"

Seriously? He really didn't know? "Seth, take a wild guess."

"I…" He was totally at a loss.

She was messing with him, and she really needed to

stop. "I'm in labor. I'm having my baby, like right now, tonight, and I wonder if—"

"Wait. What? Are you all right?" Now he really was freaked. "Is there bleeding? Do you need an ambulance?"

"No. Yes! I mean, I'm fine. There's no blood."

"But you mentioned dripping..."

"It's not blood—it's amniotic fluid. My water broke. It happens. You said you wanted to help, and I need someone to give me a ride to the hospital, and I thought—"

"Wait. You're not due for a month, you said."

"I'm at thirty-six weeks and going into labor now is perfectly normal."

"It is?"

"Believe me, if it wasn't, I'd have already called 911."

Another deep silence. And finally, "All right, then." His voice was dead calm again. Like he'd flipped a switch from frantic future step-uncle back to law-enforcement professional, a man with a job to do and no time to waste on the vagaries of human emotion. "Are you at home?"

"Yes."

"You didn't give me your address." She rattled it off. "Okay, then. Fifteen minutes, I'll be there. Did you call your doctor?"

"I will. As soon as I hang up and get through this next contrac—" A ragged yelp escaped her.

"Jody. Are you still with me?"

"Right here," she grunted.

"Are you okay?"

"Fine—except for, you know, having a baby."

"Tell me honestly. Do you need an ambulance?"

Given the pressure bearing down on her uterus, she

longed to scream, *Yes!* But she'd done this before. It felt normal, if having a baby could ever be called such a thing. "I just need a ride, okay? And I need a ride soon."

"I'm on my way."

Fourteen minutes later, she'd been through three more contractions, in between which she'd called her doctor, wiped up the dripped-on rug, put on a maxipad, yoga pants and a big shirt and carried her already-packed suitcase to the front door. Not bad for a woman in active labor.

She was crouched in the front hall, panting her way through the next contraction, when the doorbell rang. "It's open!" she shrieked and panted some more.

The door swung back, and she was looking at Seth's boots. "Jody? Are you—"

"Kind of busy here…" She waved a hand at him and went back to focusing on her breathing, on riding out the pain.

He came and knelt at her side until that one peaked and passed off.

Only then did she meet his eyes. "Thanks for coming." He wore jeans and a T-shirt and looked almost approachable.

She held out her arm. "Help me up?" He pulled her gently to her feet. She swayed against him for a moment. It was reassuring, leaning on him, such a broad, hard wall of a man. She could see the dark dots of beard stubble on his strong jaw, and he smelled clean and warm, like a just-ironed shirt. She was suddenly ridiculously glad she had called him. "Thanks."

"You ready?" He bent to grab the handle of her suitcase. "Let's go."

Outside, he led her to the camo-green Grand Chero-kee parked at the curb. "Back or front?"

"What? You didn't bring the cruiser?" When he only looked at her patiently, she answered his question. "I'll sit in back. More space for rolling around in agony when the next contraction hits."

He got her settled in, tossed her suitcase into the pas-senger seat and climbed up behind the wheel.

The ride to Justice Creek General took seven min-utes. She knew because she was timing contractions and the spaces between them the whole way.

At the hospital, they were ready for her. She'd prereg-istered and her ob-gyn, Dr. Kapur, had called ahead to say Jody was on the way. They put her in a wheelchair and rolled her to a birthing suite.

Seth followed her right in there.

"Thanks." She flashed him a pretty good imitation of a smile. "I'm good now. You can go."

"Someone should be here. I'll stay."

"But I can call—"

"It's almost three in the morning. I'm already here."

She would have argued with him, but she knew how much good that would do her. "You're staying no mat-ter what I say, aren't you?"

"That's right."

A nurse came in and introduced herself as Sandy. She took Jody's vitals, waited out another contraction with her and then got a quick history. After that, she pulled a gown and a pair of canary yellow socks with nonskid soles from a cupboard.

"Your gown and some cozy socks." Sandy handed them over and pointed at a set of long cabinets tucked into the corner. "Your street clothes can go in there. Dr. Kapur should be in soon." She nodded at Seth. "Sheriff."

"Thanks, Sandy," he replied, as though he and Sandy were best pals and he had every right to be there. Apparently, Sandy was on the same page with him. She shot him a big smile and left them alone.

"You need help getting into that?" He gestured at the gown.

"No, thanks. Step out, please."

"If you need me—"

"Thanks. I mean that. Out."

He left and she changed into the gown and socks. Dr. Kapur came. She examined Jody and confirmed what Jody already knew. Just like the first time, her baby was coming fast.

Forty-five minutes later, Jody had flown through transition, and it was time to start pushing.

Somebody had let Seth back into the room. By then, Jody didn't even care. Pushing a baby out left zero room for modesty. And privacy? Forget about it.

She had the mattress adjusted to prop up her back, her gown rucked up high and her legs spread wide, her feet in the bright yellow socks digging into the mattress. Seth was right there. He gave her his hand to hold on to.

Okay, he was practically a stranger, but so what? He was there and he was strong and steady, and she could hold on to him, right now, when she needed him.

Dignity? Self-control? She had none. She shouted and swore and clutched Seth's hand for dear life.

Was it this bad last time? It must have been. She should have remembered that.

As Marybeth's head crowned, Jody shouted, "Never

am I ever having sex again! Never in this lifetime, no matter what!"

Dr. Kapur let out a soft chuckle and told her how great she was doing, that she should push just a little bit more, bear down just a little bit harder...

And she did and she felt it—the head sliding out. Moaning in agony, she looked down between her wide-open legs as Dr. Kapur freed Marybeth's little shoulders.

And that was it. Marybeth slithered out into the world.

With another long moan of exhaustion, Jody let go of Seth's hand and let her head fall back against the pillows.

When she looked again, Seth was down there with the baby. Dr. Kapur was checking her airways. Marybeth let out a soft cry—and then a louder one.

Dr. Kapur passed Seth the blood- and vernix-streaked baby. Seth took her, held her close, whispered something Jody couldn't hear.

And then Jody was reaching for her. "Please..."

Seth passed her over, laying her down on Jody's still-giant stomach. Jody gathered her in, kissed her sticky hair, her bloodstained cheek. "Hello, Marybeth. I'm so glad you're here..."

Seth stood close to the bed where Jody held her newborn baby.

The doctor got to work cutting the cord and stitching Jody up. Jody paid no attention to what was going on between her legs. She cuddled Marybeth close and cooed in her ear. The nurse, Sandy, approached the bed with a stack of clean linens.

Seth glanced down at the streaks of blood and white stuff on his arms. He could use a little cleaning up, too. "I'll be right back," he whispered to Jody. She didn't even look up.

In the suite's bathroom, he rinsed away the blood and the milky white goo that had covered Marybeth. With a wet paper towel, he rubbed the stuff off his T-shirt, too. He leaned close to the mirror, checking for more on his face and neck.

Seth stared in his own eyes and marveled at what had just happened in the other room.

Could a moment change everything? Seth knew that it could. A moment was all it had taken seven years ago in Chicago—a single moment to empty him out to a shell of himself.

And back there in the other room, it had happened again. He'd held Nicky's baby for a matter of seconds. Those seconds made up the moment that changed his world all over again.

In the space of that moment he saw his own emptiness, and he saw it filled with all he needed, everything that mattered, right there in his arms. Life. Hope. The future. All of it in a tiny, naked, squirming newborn baby still connected to her mother by a twisted, vein-wrapped cord.

As he'd held Marybeth for the first time, the past was all around him. And not just what happened in Chicago.

But also another moment years and years ago, the first time that everything changed.

He'd been fourteen that day, the day his dad brought Seth's future stepmom, Darlene, to the Bar-Y for the first time. She'd brought her little boy with her, too.

"Nicky," she'd said, *"this is Seth..."* Seth looked

down and saw the kid looking up at him through giant blue eyes.

At that time, Seth already considered himself a grown-up. He understood life and there was nothing that great about it. He sure had no interest in his dad's new girl-friend's kid.

But then the kid in question had held out his small hand.

Seth had taken it automatically, given it a shake and then tried to let go.

But Nicky managed to catch his index finger and hold on. *"Tet,"* he said proudly. It was as close as he could get to saying *Seth* at that point.

And that was when it happened, that was the first moment when everything changed.

As Nicky clutched his finger and Darlene chuckled softly, Seth felt a warm, rising sensation in his chest, a tightness, but a good tightness. He kind of liked the little boy and his pretty mother.

He slid a glance at his dad. Bill Yancy, always so sad and lonely and serious, was smiling, too.

What would it be like, to have a mom who made his dad smile, to have a little brother who called him *Tet*? Seth realized that he wanted a chance to find out.

As soon as Darlene and Seth's dad were married, Bill legally adopted Nick. Seth finally had a normal, happy, loving family. The years that followed were good ones. The best.

But eventually there was Chicago and the next big mo-ment, the one that added up to the death of his dreams. After Chicago, Seth had come home. He'd taken a job with the sheriff's office.

But really, he'd only been going through the motions

of living. And he only felt emptier with each new loss. Five years ago they lost Darlene to breast cancer. And then his dad, sad and silent and lonely all over again, had pulled up stakes and moved to Florida.

Seth had tried to stay positive. Two years ago, he'd run for sheriff and won. He'd tried to be proud of that, of serving his community and doing a good job of it.

But losing Nicky last November had been the final straw. Since Nicky died, Seth had greeted every empty day with bleak determination to get through it and on to the next one.

Until today.

Until he held Nicky's baby, and it came to him sharply that while Nicky might be lost, this tiny, living part of him carried on.

When Seth returned to the main room, the nurse was busy at the sink near the window. The doctor was gone. Jody looked up from Marybeth and into his eyes. "Thanks. For the ride. For being here."

"Nothing to thank me for. I'm right where I want to be."

Jody started to say something.

But the nurse stepped close again. "Let's clean that little sweetie up a little." She patted Jody's shoulder. "Then we'll help you with a shower and bring on the tea and toast."

Jody surrendered Marybeth reluctantly. She let her head fall back again and closed her eyes. A long, tired sigh escaped her. "I'm beat." She looked it, her brown hair pulled back in a saggy ponytail, bruised circles beneath the lowered fans of her eyelashes.

Seth wanted to reach out, to smooth the damp hair

that had straggled loose from her ponytail. He wanted to take her hand again, to reassure her that he was good with this, with Marybeth, with all of it. That he was there for Jody to hold on to. And he was. All the way. Because being there for his brother's baby meant being there for Jody, too.

He lifted a hand toward her, but changed his mind and let it drop to his side without touching her. She looked peaceful, her head on the pillow, eyes still closed, that back-talking mouth of hers soft now, lips slightly parted. Resting. Jody deserved every second of rest she could get. He would stand watch over her, back the nurse off until she woke up.

"You should go now," she said softly without opening her eyes.

He didn't answer her.

Death had stolen Nick's right to be there for his baby. But Seth was very much alive. And whether Jody Bravo liked it or not, Seth was stepping up to give Marybeth anything—and everything—she might need.

He was going nowhere. Marybeth's mom might as well start getting used to having him around.

Chapter Four

"She is so beautiful," Elise whispered. She cradled Marybeth close and smoothed the blanket around her sleeping face. "When can you go home?"

"They're keeping us overnight. Barring complications, Dr. Kapur will release us tomorrow morning."

Elise, who'd had Jed drive her straight to the hospital from the airport, looked faintly alarmed. "What complications?"

Jody waved a hand. "There are none. Relax. It's just to be on the safe side. Both Marybeth and I are fine."

"I'm so glad. And I can't believe we all three managed to be unavailable just when you needed us."

"It happened." Jody poured herself some water from the pitcher on the bed tray and took a long sip. "And it all worked out."

"But we were supposed to—"

"Leesie, Marybeth is fine. I'm fine. You are not to feel bad about it."

"But I do. I should have been here and I—"

"Stop. How was New York?"

"Amazing. Do you need me to make some calls?"

"All done. I'm covered at Bloom, and every Bravo for miles around knows about Marybeth. Three of our brothers and their wives have been by already—oh, and Rory and Walker, too."

"You are a marvel."

"Well, I had help. Seth made most of the calls for me." Seth had left twenty minutes ago, just as Elise was arriving. Jed had gone off to get some coffee, giving the sisters a little alone time.

Elise's mouth curved in a soft little smile. "Aren't you glad you reached out to Seth?"

"Yeah. He's been great. The guy won't *stop* helping me. I keep telling him he can go."

"And now he has."

"Not for long. He'll be back at six or so, he said."

Elise frowned. "Is that okay with you?"

"It's odd. I mean, already, I'm kind of used to having him around. And he really does seem to want to be here. He's in insta-love with his niece."

Elise rocked the pink bundle gently from side to side. "Well, and who wouldn't be?"

"And he really seems to want to help. Plus, when they brought in the birth certificate he was all over it, making sure I put Nick down as Marybeth's dad."

"And here you thought he didn't even care," Elise chided.

"Yeah. I got it way wrong on that score. And I guess,

well, I don't think it hurts if he wants to be involved. Do you?"

"Of course not. But the real question is, how do *you* feel about it?"

Jody stared out the window at the thick green branches of the fir tree just beyond the glass. "It's strange, how easy it would be for me to start to count on him. He's bossy, you know? But now I'm getting used to him, he's somehow bossy in a good way. He knows what he wants and he really does try to do the right thing. And I have no problem pushing back at him when I don't like what he's up to."

Elise wore her dreamy look suddenly. "Oh, I get that. Jed's the same way. There's Jed's way and the wrong way. Most of the time he's right, but when he's not I have to stand my ground with him. And that's okay with me. Kind of keeps me on my toes." Marybeth let out a whine. "She's waking up. Look at those eyes. Gorgeous…"

"Bring her here. I'll nurse her again. I'm supposed to practice every chance I get."

Elise brought her over and settled her in Jody's waiting arms. She pushed her gown open and Marybeth rooted around, finally latching on, but not for long. After only a minute or two, she popped off the nipple and started fussing again, little, cranky bleats of sound.

Jody felt a sudden spurt of anxiety, a sense of complete incompetence. She forced herself to take a slow breath and let it out by degrees. This was new territory—she had to remember that. She'd never nursed her little boy, hadn't even let herself see his tiny face. They'd taken him away as soon as he was born. Her breasts, swollen with milk that wouldn't be used, had ached for days afterward…

"Jody? You okay?"

She blinked and shook her head. "Yeah. Sorry, faded out there for a minute."

Elise laughed. "Well, you did just have a baby. It's possible you're a little tired."

Marybeth cried louder. Jody switched her to the other side. She latched on again. That time she stuck with it awhile. Jody looked down at her little mouth, her tiny nose. *Please, God, let me do this right...*

Eventually, Marybeth fell asleep again.

Elise took her and tucked her in the bassinet. Jed came in. They visited for a few more minutes, and then he and Elise left.

The afternoon passed slowly. More family and friends came to see Marybeth, including Nell, who'd hopped a plane from Phoenix as soon as she heard the baby had been born. She said she was ready to come home anyway. Her hookup with that old friend hadn't worked out, after all.

Nell didn't stay long. Nobody did. They just wanted to check in, see the new mom and make a fuss about the baby. They all offered to be there to drive Jody and Marybeth home the next day. She thanked them and told them she'd call them if she needed a ride.

The nurses served dinner at five. Jody ate with one hand, Marybeth cradled in the other. The baby was fussing a lot, nursing fitfully but not really settling in about it. Around five thirty, she finally closed her eyes and slept again. Jody kissed her pink forehead and tucked her back into the bassinet. A few seconds later, her cell vibrated on the bed tray.

It was her mom, calling from Hawaii. In recent years, Willow Bravo spent most of her time on vacation.

"Hi, Ma."

"Darling, I got a message from Seth Yancy that you had your baby. How are you doing?"

"My baby is beautiful and healthy and we're both fine."

"I can't wait to meet her. Give her a kiss from her grandma?"

"I will."

"And so...you're on good terms with the sheriff?"

Was she implying that Jody had been on bad terms with Seth before now? With Willow, it was hard to tell. "Yes. Well, he recently found out that he was going to be an uncle. He got in touch. We...got to know each other a little. And then I went into labor last night and needed a ride to the hospital."

"What about your sisters?"

"Long story. But anyway, Seth drove me here and then stuck around to help."

"And you are *letting* him help. This is a first."

Jody felt her stomach knot up. "Passive-aggressive much?" She was careful to speak just above a whisper in order not to wake Marybeth.

"It's only an observation," Willow answered, her voice downright gentle. "You've always been so independent— that's all I meant. It's rare for you to let someone close, especially in this sort of situation."

"What sort of situation do you mean, exactly?"

"Jody. I only mean you've never had much contact with Sheriff Yancy until very recently. This is a challenging time for you, as it is for any new mother. Usually, when things are tough for you, you don't want anyone close enough to see your weakness, especially not a man you don't know all that well."

"I'm not weak."

Willow chuckled. "You're making my point for me. You realize that, right?"

Okay, so her mother could sometimes be way too perceptive. Jody tamped down her defensiveness. "Seth is a good guy, and he's already crazy about Marybeth."

"I'm glad," said her mother in a neutral tone. Apparently, she really didn't want to fight, and Jody probably ought to stop being annoyed with her just on principle. "And I'm here if you need me."

Right. In Hawaii, Jody was careful *not* to say. And then she felt guilty for even thinking that. Willow *had* flown to Sacramento all those years ago because she was worried about her older daughter. When she'd discovered Jody's secret, she'd stayed long enough to meet the childless couple who would be taking the baby. Jody had called her when she went into labor, and Willow had flown right back to her side, staying with her through the birth and recovery. So really, Willow *had* been there when Jody needed her.

"Thanks, Ma," Jody said and found that she meant it. "And when *are* you coming home?"

"Right away, if you need me."

"No, really. I'm doing fine."

"A few weeks, then."

"All right. Have a great time."

"I will. And I…"

"What, Ma?"

"I wasn't the most attentive mother. I realize that." It was only the truth. For the first eighteen years of Jody's life, Willow was laser-focused on getting her lover, Jody's father, to divorce his first wife and make Willow his bride. "But I do love you, darling," she said. "Very much."

"And I love you." It was true. Willow could get on her last nerve, and Jody hated that her own mother had spent a couple of decades trying to steal another woman's husband. But she'd worked past that bitterness, mostly. And her siblings and half siblings had, too.

They chatted a little longer about inconsequential things, and then Willow said goodbye.

Seth returned a few minutes later wearing jeans and a different T-shirt. He had an overnight bag in one hand and a pie in the other.

Jody's heart kind of lifted at the sight of him. She realized she'd been waiting for him, that she'd wanted him to come back, that he made her feel safe and cared for. And she liked that—though she'd always been a person who insisted on taking care of herself.

Her pleasure at seeing him was probably some weird postpartum reaction. She decided not to analyze it too deeply. "Oh, look. You brought me a pie. Key lime?"

He almost smiled. "How'd you guess?"

"I'm a girl who knows her pies. One of your admirers made it, am I right?"

He half scowled as he set the pie on the low cabinet near the door. "They're very nice women. And how did you know about them?"

"Seth. Everybody knows about your fan club. It's a thing. People find it charming that the sheriff has lots of female admirers."

He cleared his throat officiously. And his ears were pink, which she was coming to realize was the way that he blushed. Seth Yancy, a blusher. She loved that. "You're grinning," he grumbled. "Why?"

"You really want to know?"

"Never mind." He set his bag down on the floor

near the cabinet and approached the bassinet. "How's our girl?"

Our girl. Should it bother her that he thought of Marybeth as partly his?

Well, if it should, it didn't. Not really. Instead, she found his claiming of her daughter charming. Like his fan club and the cute way he blushed.

"Jody?"

"Um?"

"How's she been?" he whispered, bending over the sleeping Marybeth.

"So far, so good. A little fussy. Everybody says she's gorgeous."

"Because she is." Reluctantly, he straightened. "I want to pick her up."

"Don't you dare. Let her sleep. And you'll get your chance before you know it. It won't be long before she's awake again, believe me." He was looking at her so… steadily. "What?"

He took the chair by the bed. "You look tired. Did you get any sleep?"

"Please. People in and out constantly. Marybeth fussing. Trying to learn how to nurse her. It goes on…"

He peered over at the baby again. "She seems peaceful now."

"Let's enjoy it while it lasts. And I have to ask, what's with the overnight bag?"

He glanced at it as though he hadn't noticed until now that he'd carried it in with him. "Oh, that. I talked to the nurse a few minutes ago."

"About?"

"I had to promise her some of your pie, but they'll be bringing in a cot for me in a little while."

She knew she absolutely, positively ought to draw the line at this. "You think you're sleeping in this room with me?"

His big shoulders slumped. "Look. All right. If it's too much, I can camp out in the waiting room."

"Seth. Marybeth is fine. You should just go home."

A muscle twitched in his rocklike jaw. "It's just one night. I'll feel better if I'm here. They won't let me have a cot out in the waiting room, but I'll just sleep in a chair out there…" And he looked at her through those gorgeous eyes that were a warm brown with golden flecks near the iris. Oh, God. He was so working her. "I want to be here in the morning. I want to take you back to your house, help you get settled in…"

Before she could make herself form the word *no*, there was a tap on the door.

An orderly stuck his head in. "We have your rollaway."

And just like that, it was decided. Seth jumped up to help, and Jody didn't say a word to stop him.

It wasn't so bad, having him in the room with her through the night. He made himself useful, getting up more than once to quiet the baby when she cried, even changing her diaper twice. And the next morning, he went to Jody's house to pick up a few things for her while she waited for Dr. Kapur to release her and Marybeth.

He came back with the car seat, which he'd correctly installed in the passenger-side second-row seat of his big Jeep. He'd even figured out how to put in the soft newborn insert so that Marybeth fit in there just right, all cozy and safe.

He helped Jody up into the passenger seat and then

he drove them home. Once there, he took charge, getting
Jody and the baby all comfy in Jody's room. By then it
was almost noon. He made sandwiches and heated up
some canned soup and ate lunch with Jody before heading off to the sheriff's office to get a little work done.

At six thirty, he returned with takeout from Romano's—
best Italian in town.

"Seth, you don't have to bring food. My sisters are
handling all the meals for the first few days. Elise
dropped by while you were at the justice center. She
brought her famous roast chicken and browned potatoes."

"Great," Seth replied as he loaded lasagna onto plates
for them. "We'll have the chicken tomorrow night."

He also brought a foil-wrapped pan of sinfully delicious Samoa cheesecake bars that someone in his fan
club had whipped up for him. Jody ate three of those.

"Don't bring any more desserts into my house," she
grumbled as she reached for that third bar. "Or I'll never
lose this baby weight."

"Whatever you say, Jody." Already, she knew what
he meant by that. She could dole out instructions to her
heart's content. And he would go ahead and do things
his way.

That night, he slept on the blow-up bed in her tiny
third bedroom. She shouldn't have let him. But he asked
her so nicely, and he was so great with Marybeth. In the
morning before he left, he made her oatmeal with rai-
sins and honey.

It was nice, having him fix breakfast and put it in
front of her.

"Thanks, Seth. I know I keep saying that, but you
really have gone above and beyond."

He sent her an oblique glance. "I want to ask you something, but I don't want to piss you off."

She enjoyed a bite of oatmeal. "I'm worn-out and cranky. You know that, right?"

"I think that any way I answer that is going to be wrong."

"What I meant was, good thinking on the part about not pissing me off." To that, he shrugged and sipped his coffee, and she was suddenly sure that, whatever it was, he'd decided not to ask. That was when she realized that she *wanted* him to ask. "Go ahead. What is it?"

"About you and Nicky…" He dipped up a bite of the hot cereal and brought it to his mouth. Once he'd swallowed, he muttered gruffly, "What happened with that?"

Ugh. He was such a straight-and-narrow kind of guy. She doubted he was going to think much of her answer. "How about this? I'm not mad at you for asking. And I want you to try not to get mad when I answer."

She expected him to waffle on that. But he only said, "Deal."

So she told him about that night in August. "I hadn't been out with anyone in a while—a few years, as a matter of fact."

"Why not?"

No way she felt up to going into all that right then. "Do you want to hear about what happened with your brother or not?"

He saluted her with his coffee mug. "Sorry. Go ahead."

"I decided I needed to get out more, have a little more fun in my life. So on a hot night last August, I went to Alicia's." The roadhouse was out on the state high-

way, about five miles from town. "I had a great time.
Danced a lot. Drank too much. And met your brother,
who was sweet and charming and a really good dancer.
Things just...took their natural course. We got a room
in the motel across from the roadhouse and spent the
night together."

He was watching her too closely.

Her throat felt tight, and she gulped to loosen it. "And,
yes, we used condoms. And it was just that one night."

Seth sat back in his chair. The room was too quiet.
She almost wished Marybeth would wake up and start
crying. She could go soothe her baby and stop talking
about Nick.

But Marybeth slept on. And Jody continued, "I liked
him a lot. But honestly, he was too young for me. And I
don't mean just in years. He was...such a sweetheart. So
open and true. I felt a thousand years old around him."

"Why? You're not *that* much older."

Jody chuckled. "Thanks. I think." She fiddled with
her spoon. "As for why, it was just the way I felt, that's
all—older than Nick in a thousand different ways."
Yeah, there was more to the why of it. But all that was
another story, *her* story, a story she didn't feel like sharing. "Nick wanted to go out with me and I was flat-
tered, but I knew it wasn't going anywhere. He was a
good guy, though, and we became friends. We'd hang
out together here. And at the ranch. But we never got
romantic again."

Seth sat forward. "He didn't tell me about the baby.
But he did say he wanted for there to be more with you."

"Well, that wasn't happening. Not for me. And when
I found out I was pregnant..." That had been awful. The

stick had turned blue, and she'd had to face the fact that she'd done it again.

"When you found out you were pregnant, what?"

"Come to think of it, didn't we cover that already— on the first day you came into Bloom to ask me if my baby was Nick's?"

"You mean, that you went to him right away with the news?"

"Yeah. He wanted marriage. I didn't. But we agreed we would learn how to be parents to our baby without being married. And then, way too soon, he died."

"And…that's it? That's all of it?" He glowered at her.

At least, she thought he was glowering. "Yeah. That's all—and remember, you said you would try not to get mad."

"I'm not mad."

"Well, Seth. You *look* mad."

"I miss him, that's all." His voice was like gravel rubbing on sandpaper, and those gold flecks in his eyes shone extra bright. "He and his mother were the heart of our family."

Jody felt the pressure of tears at the back of her throat. "I'm so sorry," she whispered. It sounded limp and inadequate, but what else could she say?

He pushed his chair back and picked up his empty bowl. "Thanks. For telling me. You finished?"

She passed him her bowl.

That evening at six thirty, he appeared on her doorstep again.

She was way too glad to see him. He made her life easier, putting the dinner on, washing up afterward, bringing amazing baked goods that she really should stop eating. He was always ready to help with the baby.

And there was just something so rock-solid about him. He was too serious, and half the time she just knew he was thinking unflattering things about her. But still, he made her feel safe and protected, as though nothing could go too far wrong as long as he was nearby. Already, they seemed to have fallen seamlessly into a daily routine.

The next morning, Friday, he made breakfast again. And when he left for work, she found herself wondering how she would get along when he stopped coming back.

Marybeth fussed constantly. To Jody, it seemed she must be hungry, though Jody's milk had already come down. It was whitish in color, no longer the yellowish colostrum babies got the first few days after birth. So the milk was there, but Marybeth just didn't seem to be getting enough.

Jody called the nursing coach that Dr. Kapur had recommended. The coach, Debbie, came out to the house and worked with her, giving her pointers on how to make sure Marybeth latched on properly, showing her the best nursing positions, helping her set up her rocking recliner with pillows and everything she needed close by for convenience and ease. So she would be relaxed, so Marybeth would feel safe and cozy and keep at it long enough to fill her little tummy.

Debbie's visit didn't help. That weekend was awful. Marybeth cried all the time, and Jody tried not to cry right along with her. Jody's breasts felt knotted and achy with milk, and she was already considering pumping and then feeding Marybeth her breast milk in a bottle.

But Debbie had urged Jody to give it time.

"Marybeth is doing fine," Debbie had said. "Sometimes it takes several days before mother and baby get comfortable with the nursing process."

Jody wasn't comfortable. And judging by all the wailing, neither was her baby girl. Still, she stuck with it, but she worried constantly that her baby was starving. Plus, the endless crying made her want to scream.

She was supposed to be doing it right this time.

And she wasn't. Her little baby was miserable and Jody was, too.

Thank God for Seth. He continued to sleep on the blow-up bed in the spare room. Both Saturday and Sunday, he went off to the justice center, but only for a few hours each day. Sunday, he drove out to the Bar-Y, too—and came back with a big suitcase full of his clothes.

The sight of that suitcase really lifted Jody's spirits. If he was bringing more clothes, then that meant he intended to keep camping out at her house for a while. Right?

Was it wrong to be ridiculously happy about that?

Really, she ought to tell him he didn't need to spend every free second helping her take care of her baby, that he should go home to the Bar-Y and relax at night instead of walking the floor with a squalling newborn.

But she told him no such thing. Instead, when he showed up with that suitcase, she gave him the old dresser in the spare room and told him the closet in there was his, too.

And then Marybeth started crying.

Seth put off unpacking to settle her down. By now, it seemed to Jody that Marybeth only stopped crying when Seth rocked her in his big arms.

Monday morning when he went out the door headed

for the sheriff's office, she almost grabbed his arm and begged him not to go.

After he left, Clara, who'd recovered from the flu by then, stopped by. Marybeth bawled through her visit. Clara held her anyway and said she was beautiful and reassured Jody that everything would be fine.

But everything wasn't fine. Marybeth was suffering, probably starving.

That afternoon, Jody called the nursing coach again. Debbie showed up a half an hour later. She gave Jody a few more tips for soothing Marybeth and then ran through the nursing pointers a second time, adding some relaxation exercises for the stressed-out mom to do while the baby napped. As if.

Debbie said the baby was healthy, and there was nothing to worry about. She asked for a quick rundown of Jody's diet and then declared that Jody hadn't mentioned any foods or beverages that might affect Jody's breast milk and be irritating to Marybeth's delicate system. Debbie wanted to know how many wet-diaper changes Marybeth needed in a twenty-four-hour period. When Jody said four or so, Debbie said that was normal.

Next they talked about Marybeth's poop. Because when you had a little baby, poop mattered. Debbie said one bowel movement a day at this point was normal, too, that Jody just needed to keep working with the process and give it a few more days. Things would settle down. Debbie guaranteed that.

"And call anytime." She gave Jody a blithe smile as she went out the door.

"I will." Jody nodded obediently while screaming inside.

Marybeth did go to sleep eventually. Jody put her in her bassinet and turned on the monitor. In the great room, she tried a few of her new relaxation exercises. Did they help? Not really. That Marybeth might wake up any minute and start crying again kept her on edge.

So she gave up trying to relax and checked in with Lois at Bloom to make sure everything was on track there. When she hung up with Lois, she took a load of laundry from the dryer. A single cry erupted from the baby monitor as Jody started to fold a tiny pink polka-dot shirt. Clutching the shirt to her chest, she held her breath and waited, praying Marybeth would just go back to sleep.

But the cries continued, getting louder and more insistent.

Jody tossed the little shirt in the laundry basket, grabbed the basket and took it to her bedroom. She emptied the pile of laundry on the bed, dropped the basket on the floor and bent over the bassinet.

"Shh, now. It's okay..."

Marybeth screwed up her red face and wailed all the louder.

Jody picked her up and carried her to her nursing chair.

After Marybeth had nursed, Jody burped her, changed her and even sang to her. That seemed to work, which completely surprised Jody, who couldn't carry a tune if her life depended on it. But Marybeth seemed to like the sound of Jody's voice. She settled down and relaxed against Jody's shoulder.

For a little while.

By six, she was fussing again, and Jody couldn't wait for Seth to arrive.

And by quarter of seven, when he still hadn't shown, she wanted to knock herself out with a hammer. Anything to get away from her little baby's misery and her own complete failure to be the mom she had promised herself she would be this time.

Last time, she'd done what she had to do. She'd given up her little boy. But this time, with Marybeth…

This time was her second chance.

And this time, she'd been so certain she was going to do it right.

But she wasn't doing it right. It wasn't working out. It was all going wrong.

Seth finally appeared at twenty after seven with a giant bag of Romano's takeout in one hand and a clear plastic cake caddy containing a gorgeous chocolate cake in the other. Jody wanted to shove the baby at him, grab the cake and run howling out the door.

Instead, she held her crying child on her shoulder and followed him to the kitchen, where he set the food on the counter and explained, "I'm sorry I'm late. Little family dispute. The parties involved demanded to talk to the sheriff personally before they would put down their weapons."

"Weapons!" Jody repeated in alarm, causing Marybeth to cry louder. Jody lowered her voice. "They had weapons?"

"Don't get excited. I drove out there. We talked. They put away their guns and agreed to get some family counseling. Crisis resolved." He stepped to the sink to wash his hands.

Jody experienced a moment's relief that no one was hurt. But Marybeth just kept on crying—louder than ever if that was even possible. Jody's frustration and hopelessness came flooding back. In a second or two, she would break, blow it completely, collapse to the floor wailing as loud as the baby.

Seth said the magic words. "Here. Let me take her."

The tears were pushing, demanding she let them flow. Her throat ached with the effort to hold them back. *Failure*, mocked an evil voice in her head. *You're a pitiful excuse for a mother.*

Seth was watching her. Even with her vision blurred by held-back tears, she could see his concern. Clearly, he got that she was losing it. "Jody." He put up both hands and patted the air between them, and she felt worse than ever. The poor guy not only faced angry families with guns at work, he came home to Marybeth's incompetent mom having a meltdown. "Jody, it's okay…"

"No, Seth. No, it is not okay." She had to get out of there. "Just take her. Please." Lifting Marybeth off her shoulder, she handed her over.

Seth took her in those big, gentle hands of his. As soon as he had her, before he could say one more word, Jody whirled on her heel and ran for her room, where she swung the door shut harder than she should have and gave the privacy lock a vicious twist.

Alone at last.

Sagging back against the door, she willed herself to pull it together.

But the tears kept pushing. They were going to get out. She just couldn't keep swallowing them down.

Letting her knees buckle, she sank to the floor and slammed both hands over her mouth, as if that could keep the tears from escaping.

It couldn't. *She* couldn't.

So she leaped to her feet again and marched to the bed. Shoving aside the tangle of unfolded laundry, she threw herself down with a hard, hopeless sob.

Chapter Five

It took Seth a while to get Marybeth settled. He walked a path from the kitchen to the great room and back again, bouncing her just a little with each step, creating a rhythm, a combination of movements, that usually worked to quiet her down.

As he walked her, he rubbed her tiny back, stroked his hand over the peach fuzz on her little head and whispered to her. He called her his girl, the best girl, the sweetest girl around.

The crying got weaker, then became intermittent, interspersed with hiccups. Slowly, the hiccups stopped, too.

Finally, with a tired little sigh, she went quiet.

A few cooing sounds, another sigh…and silence.

He carried her to the room he slept in and shut the curtains to block out what was left of the daylight. Then he put her down on her back on the blow-up bed, arranging pillows on either side of her to make sure she couldn't somehow wiggle over near the edge.

She was sleeping peacefully, innocent as an angel.

Now, to find out what was up with Jody.

The three bedrooms in the house were grouped together on a small L-shaped hallway off the front entry. He left the door open to his room. If Marybeth cried, he would be able to hear her. Jody's room was only a few steps away.

He tapped on her door. "Jody?" No response. He tried to decide whether to knock again or leave her alone. But then the door slowly opened.

Puffy eyes and a red nose gave her away. She wasn't crying now, but she had been.

"You okay?"

"Not really." She smoothed back her tangled hair and slid a glance over his shoulder, toward the other two bedrooms. "Is she...?"

"Sound asleep. I put her on my bed and boxed her in with pillows. She's never been in that pretty room you made for her, right?"

Jody sniffled. She rubbed at her nose with a wadded-up tissue. "Right."

"So I didn't put her down in there."

"Um. Okay."

"I thought maybe if she woke up in a strange room, she might be scared or something."

Jody made a strangled sound—a wild laugh, maybe. Or a tortured sob. He couldn't really tell which. "You're amazing, you know that? You're ten times the mother I'll ever be."

He had no idea how to respond to that, so he went with, "You're a fine mother."

Apparently, his reply amused her. She let out a tight little laugh—which was great, he decided. He would take amusement over a breakdown any day. She asked, "And you've determined this, how?"

He didn't even have to think it over. "You're here for her. You want what's good for her. It's obvious you love her and will do anything for her."

"It is?" Her voice was so small. Lost-sounding.

He knew she needed comforting. And he was there to do whatever she and Marybeth needed. He held out his arms. "Come here."

She didn't even hesitate, only swayed toward him with a sigh. He gathered her in. They stood there in the open doorway to her room, arms wrapped around each other. He breathed in her coconut-and-vanilla scent from the lotion she used on Marybeth and tried not to think too hard about how good her body felt pressed close to his.

"I should pull myself together," she mumbled against his shoulder. "But you're kind of good to lean on."

"Lean all you want. Whenever you need to." He rubbed his chin against her silky hair, realized that was going a bit far and stopped.

"I was so sure," she whispered, pressing herself even closer against him, her voice low enough that he could barely make out the words. "I had it all planned. I was going to do it right this time around."

He remembered what she'd blurted out concerning first and second babies the night Marybeth was born. It was probably none of his business. Unless she needed to talk about it. In that case, he was more than willing to listen.

Stroking a hand down her back, he echoed, "*This time around.* Meaning there was a time before?"

Jody lifted her head from his shoulder and looked up into his stern, square-jawed face.

What was it about him? At first, she'd only wanted him to leave her alone. But now she couldn't even imagine how she would have survived the past week without him. She couldn't wait for him to show up at the end of each day. It meant so much to know he was right there in the spare room every night, ready to pitch in whenever she needed him.

She held his gaze. "You already know there was a time before."

He answered with a slow nod. "You want to tell me about it?"

Did she? "Yeah. And to work up the courage, I'm going to need cake. Lots and lots of cake."

He lifted a hand. His fingers ghosted down her temple and guided a stray curl behind her ear, the light touch warming her through and through. "You have to eat your lasagna and Caesar salad first."

"Oh, now. There's a real hardship."

He actually smiled then, and it looked really good on him. "Excellent. We have a plan."

With a lot more reluctance than she wanted to admit to, she pressed her hands to his broad chest and stepped back. His arms dropped away. She went to the nightstand and got him the baby monitor. "The receiver's already in the kitchen."

He took it and turned for his room.

* * *

Jody ate her dinner and had her cake. By the time they carried their plates to the sink, she was half hoping Marybeth would wake up and give her an excuse not to rehash old news.

But her daughter slept on.

They went into the great room and sat on the couch together—Jody at one end, Seth on the other. She tucked her stocking feet up on the cushions and tried to decide where to start.

Seth waited, not pushing her.

Finally, she began, "During my last year of high school, I got pregnant by my high school sweetheart..." At three months along, right after graduation, she'd finally worked up the nerve to tell him. "He went ballistic, accused me of trying to pass some other guy's baby off as his. And then he packed up and moved to Indiana. He was already registered at Notre Dame for the fall."

Seth muttered something under his breath.

"What?" she asked.

"Never mind. Go on."

She pulled a throw pillow from behind her back, braced it on the sofa arm and leaned her elbow on it as she explained how crazy things had been with her family then. "My dad's first wife, Sondra, had just died. The day after the funeral, he married my mother and moved her, Nell and me into the mansion he'd built for Sondra. Elise still lived there at the time and so did her best friend, Tracy, who'd been taken in by Sondra when Tracy's parents died. Elise was reeling from the loss of her mom—and then in moves her dad's husband-stealing new wife and two of the kids she'd had by him."

"Bad?"

"Unbearable. We're all close now. We've put all the old garbage behind us. But at the time, Elise and Tracy hated Nell and me, and we hated them right back. We all resented my mother for being a total home wrecker. There were fights, screaming matches. I only lived there for two months and then I moved out again. I told everyone I couldn't take all the drama..."

"But really, it was because of the baby?"

"Yeah. But I didn't tell anyone—not anyone in my family, not any of my friends. I just couldn't deal with talking about it, somehow. I was eighteen, so nobody had to know." She'd found an adoption agency who tracked down her runaway boyfriend in Indiana. "My ex-boyfriend signed off all rights to the baby. Then the agency found me the Levinsons, a really wonderful couple in Sacramento. The Levinsons paid all of my expenses. They flew me to Sacramento and put me up in my own apartment. I had all the money I needed for living expenses during the remainder of my pregnancy. They also made sure that I had the best prenatal care."

"Nobody in your family wondered why you'd suddenly moved to California?" He sounded skeptical.

"It was a hard time for the family. My half siblings were totally pissed off at how my dad married Willow so fast and installed her in Sondra's house. None of us—meaning my mother's kids—liked it, either. My moving to Sacramento for a while didn't even make the radar with them. Except for my mother. She's usually the definition of self-absorbed, but somehow she figured it out. I was six months along when she showed up on my doorstep. She didn't give me a hard time, just wanted to know how I was and insisted on meeting the Levinsons. She's never told anyone, as far as I know."

"It's a secret, then—from everyone else in your family?"

A curl of defensiveness tightened her belly. "It's just… It's never been something anyone needed to know."

"That wasn't a criticism." He looked at her so levelly, and his voice was kind. "I just needed to know if the information is confidential."

"I *am* going to tell them. One of these days." She glanced toward the unlit fireplace and tried not to feel like crap about everything.

After a minute or two, he nudged her along. "So… you had the baby?"

She just wanted this sad, old story over with. "Yeah. A little boy. The Levinsons took him right away. I didn't want to see him or hold him, you know? Didn't want to take any chance of getting too attached. The Levinsons and I agreed *not* to keep in touch. When he's eighteen, if he chooses to, he can contact me. I moved back home a few weeks after the birth. That should have been the end of it. But then, about two years ago, I couldn't take it anymore, wondering. Worrying that I'd done the wrong thing, that maybe he was unhappy, maybe he needed me."

"You got in touch with the couple who adopted him, after all?"

She shook her head. "I didn't want to freak them out, get them scared that I had changed my mind. I just wanted to know for sure that he was all right. So I hired a private investigator. He worked up a detailed report, including pictures of the Levinson family with my little boy, whose name is Josh. I could see from the photographs that he's happy. There was one of him hugging his mother in the front yard…" The pointless tears blurred her vision again. She dashed them away. "All that to say that I believe Josh Levinson is doing just fine."

Seth grabbed the box of tissues from the coffee table. He held them out to her.

She took one and blew her nose for the umpteenth time that evening. "And now…"

"Yeah?"

"Well, the plan was that this time, with Marybeth, I would do it right, you know? I would keep my baby and have it all handled. I would be calm and relaxed and completely on top of things."

"That's a tall order."

"A lot of women manage it."

"Jody, you're doing fine."

"But Marybeth seems so unhappy. I mean, am I starving her? It seems like she's hungry all the time. So far it just feels like I'm getting everything wrong." She lowered her head and tore at the soggy tissue in her hands.

"Hey." Seth's hand settled over hers, so warm, slightly rough, wonderfully soothing.

She looked up on a ragged breath and met those surprisingly soft brown eyes of his. Had she expected him to judge her?

Maybe. A little—after all, he was such a straight-and-narrow, upstanding sort of a guy.

But Seth didn't judge. "Your high school sweetheart was clearly no hero, and you did what you had to do at the time. You even checked back later to make sure the child was all right. And you're not getting it wrong now. Marybeth is healthy. She's going to be fine. You need to stop being so hard on yourself."

Jody sniffed. "Thank you." She probably shouldn't have, but she let her body sway toward him.

He didn't pull back. On the contrary, he wrapped those big arms around her and gave her a hug. For a lovely, lingering moment, she leaned into his solid strength, breathed in his clean scent and allowed herself to feel completely safe and protected.

And then a series of fussy little cries started up from the baby monitor.

"Shh," he whispered, his breath warm against her hair. "Maybe we'll get lucky and she'll go back to sleep."

"We can hope." She shamelessly indulged herself and snuggled in closer.

But the cries from the monitor only increased in length and intensity. Reluctantly, Jody pulled free of his embrace. She dabbed up the rest of her tears.

"I'll get her," he said.

She managed a smile. "You're the best. But it's definitely my turn."

It really helped, Jody realized, to confide in Seth, to let him reassure her and comfort her.

Within the next couple of days, the nursing seemed to go better. Marybeth still cried, but not nearly so much. She finally seemed to be getting enough milk.

By the end of that week, Jody knew she should tell Seth he didn't need to stay over anymore, that she could manage just fine on her own. But Sunday was Mother's Day, the biggest flower-selling day of the year—with the possible exception of Valentine's Day.

When she mentioned the crushing workload at Bloom over that coming weekend, Seth took family leave from the justice center. He looked after Marybeth full-time on Thursday, Friday, Saturday and Mother's Day, so that Jody could run between the house and Bloom getting ready for the big day and then selling flowers like crazy when Sunday finally came.

She promised herself that on Monday, once the Mother's Day push was over, she would sit down and have a talk with Seth. She would tell him how much she appreciated all he'd done and suggest that the time had come for him to move back to the ranch.

But Monday came and went. Somehow, she never quite got around to reminding him that she didn't need him living in her spare room anymore.

So he continued to show up every evening bringing wonderful baked goods from his fans at the sheriff's office and spelling Jody with Marybeth. He went back to the ranch once or twice a week to check in with the couple who took care of the place. But he lived at Jody's, essentially. And she just let him.

Because he took such good care of her little girl—and of Jody, too, to be honest. She counted on him more than she should have. Her life went so smoothly when he was around.

And sometimes, in the evenings while Marybeth slept, they would stream a movie together or just sit and talk about nothing in particular—like what went on at the sheriff's office and how his dad liked living in Dunedin, Florida, and how her mother had seemed driven to travel constantly since her father had died.

So yeah. When he left, she would not only miss his help with Marybeth, she would miss his company, too.

Elise, Nell, Clara and her half brother Darius's new wife, Ava, all stopped by that week. When they teased Jody that the sheriff had fallen for her, she shook her head and explained how Seth just needed to be there for Nick's little girl.

By then, Jody was taking Marybeth with her to Bloom for a few hours each day and feeling more and more confident that she hadn't turned out to be a complete failure at motherhood, after all. Really, it wasn't fair to Seth the way she kept taking advantage of him. The guy had his own life. How could he get out there and live it when he spent every spare moment with her and her baby?

Friday morning at breakfast, she made herself broach the subject. "Friday already," she said, going for a light touch. "Can you believe it?"

He sent her one of those looks. Like he could tell from her voice that she was probably up to something. "I've noticed it generally comes after Thursday."

"What I meant was, maybe you want a night off for once. You could catch a movie, go out for a beer…"

He frowned and then he shrugged. "I can watch a movie here with you, and there's beer in the fridge."

Okay, so much for the offhand approach. She wiped her mouth with her napkin. "Fine, Seth. I'll be more direct."

"Good idea." He watched her, those gold-flecked eyes wary.

"You've been here every night since we brought Marybeth home from the hospital…"

He set down his coffee cup. "You want me to get my stuff together and go back to the ranch, is that it?"

"No, I… Seth, I love having you here. I honestly do.

You're incredible with Marybeth and you're always so helpful, and I enjoy your company, too."

"So what's the problem, then?"

"Nothing. There's no problem. It's just, well, you've been beyond wonderful, but you have your own life and I have mine. We can't just go on like this, with you living in my spare room indefinitely."

"Why not? I like it here. I like everything about living here. I like helping out, being with Marybeth. And as you said, you and I get along great."

"But I—"

"Wait a minute." Now he was scowling. "Is it that you're afraid people will talk?"

She laughed. She couldn't help it.

His scowl deepened. "Why is that funny?"

"I don't know. I mean, who even worries about stuff like that anymore?"

His ears turned red. "I do. And if it bothers you, I—"

"Seth. Any possible gossip about you and me is not a problem for me, I promise you."

"Do you want me to pay rent, then?" Muscles bulged and knotted as he lifted an arm to rub the back of his big neck. "Because I'm happy to pay rent. In fact, I've been thinking I really should contribute. How about six hundred a month? Would that be enough?"

"Don't be ridiculous. Of course you're not paying me rent. You buy most of the food. You take care of the baby. You cook. You clean." She flopped back in her chair and folded her arms across her stomach. "Oh, Seth. Rent? Excuse me? Uh-uh. No way."

He got up, got the coffeepot and poured himself another cup. She watched him and tried not to think about how much she would miss him when he was gone, miss these ordinary moments—having breakfast together, watching him get up for more coffee, admiring the way he filled out his uniform both going and coming.

Yeah, okay. So what if she was perving on him? She might have sworn off sex and men, but there was no law against enjoying the view.

He sat back down. "All right. You like having me here. I make things easier for you, and you and I get along. You've refused my offer of rent and you say you're not worried about what people might say. So then, if none of those things are a problem for you, why *do* you want me to go back to the ranch?"

She gave up and admitted the truth. "I don't."

He got that look men too often get when confronted with the workings of a woman's mind. "Then, Jody, why are we talking about this?"

"Because… I don't know. I feel that I'm taking advantage of you."

"You're not. Can we consider this subject closed? Please."

"But…don't you want, you know, your freedom? Your independence? You're a single guy, and you ought to be enjoying yourself."

"Enjoying myself doing what, exactly?"

"I don't know. Playing poker with the guys? Going out with superhot women? Staying up all night?"

The corner of his stern mouth twitched. For Seth, the slight shift in expression was almost a grin. "I can stay up all night here. And I do. Whenever Marybeth won't go to sleep."

"Oh, you are just hilarious," she said with a sneer.

He knocked back a big slug of coffee and set the cup down harder than he needed to. "Look. Poker, sex with strange women and staying up all night have never been things that held much appeal for me. I'm a family guy, but my chance for getting married and having kids... well, that didn't work out for me."

"Hold on. Didn't work out? What does that mean?"

He rubbed the back of his neck again. "There was someone, once. Her name was Irene Vargas. She died."

When had that happened? She'd never heard a thing about it. "Here in Justice Creek?"

"No. Before. Years ago. In Chicago. I went to college there, and then I went to work for Chicago PD."

"Wait. You fell in love in Chicago and she died?"

"Yeah."

"Oh, Seth." What was it about him? He was so straight-up, so serious, so emotionally guarded. He wouldn't give his heart easily. That he'd loved someone and lost her—that would have cut him so deep. "I don't know what to say."

He made a gruff, throat-clearing sound. "There's nothing *to* say."

Oh, yes, there was. She wanted to know about it—about Irene, his lost love. All the details. Everything. But he was wearing his blank-eyed, watchful, lawman stare, and she knew he'd already revealed more than he wanted to. Still, she couldn't stop herself from suggesting, "I just meant, how are you going to find someone else if you're hanging around here all the time?"

"I'm not looking for anyone else."

"But—"

"Look, Jody. You're on your own and so am I. We get along and we both love Marybeth. I would rather be here than anywhere else. If you don't mind me being here, would you please not tell me that I should go?"

Okay, she got the message. He really wanted to be here. And *she* liked having him here. Win/win. Right?

Too bad warning bells had started ringing in the back of her brain. Because she liked having him here a little *too* much, now, didn't she? He was kind and smart—and funny in his dry, serious way. He took really good care of her daughter and of her. Add to all that the undeniable fact that he looked way too good in his uniform...

If she let him keep staying here, who knew what unacceptable emotions might creep up on her? He could be dangerous to her, to her heart that had already been broken and broken again, thank you very much.

And yet...

He loved her daughter, and he was a rock, right there when she needed him. She owed him for all the ways he'd come through for her since the night Marybeth was born.

At this point, she just couldn't bring herself to insist that he go. "All right, then, Seth. You're welcome to stay. We'll just take it day by day. If one of us starts to feel differently about this arrangement, we'll reevaluate. How's that?"

His hint of a smile went full out, and her silly heart did a somersault in the cage of her chest. "Thanks, Jody. You've made me a happy man."

Chapter Six

All that day and into the evening Jody couldn't stop asking herself, *Am I falling for Seth?*

Uh-uh. No way.

It was only that he'd turned out to somehow be the perfect man for her at this point in her life. All hot and hunky—and his idea of a great time was changing diapers and sleeping on her blow-up bed.

Was that even normal?

The guy really needed to get out more.

And seriously. Given the circumstances, of course he would start to seem like the guy for her. He adored her child, treated Jody like a queen and lived in her house with her, ensuring that she got an eyeful of his broad chest and fine butt day in and day out.

No, she decided late that night as she sat in her nursing chair with Marybeth in her arms. She wasn't falling for Seth. She was just grateful to him. Grateful and appreciative of his many wonderful qualities.

As any woman in her position would be.

The fourth Tuesday in May, Jody packed up Marybeth and all her baby gear and drove to Bloom at nine thirty in the morning. Marybeth behaved like an angel that day, so Jody stayed on past her usual few hours. Customer traffic was high for a Tuesday, with steady sales all morning and into the afternoon.

At four, Marybeth cooed from her carrier on the design counter as Jody filled a large Murano glass vase with purple irises and red tulips for a regular customer.

Marlie, at the register ringing up a sale, looked up when the entry bell chimed. "I'll be right with you…"

"No hurry," said the customer. She was probably around Jody's age, slim and attractive, with gorgeous, long ash-blond hair. She spotted Jody right away. They shared a smile, and the woman wandered over to the design counter.

"What a darling baby," she said. As if on cue, Marybeth cooed and waved her tiny hands.

Jody chuckled. "She can be an angel, absolutely. You have kids?"

"No." The blonde looked kind of wistful. "Still single, no babies." And then she asked much too casually, "Are you Jody?"

Jody clipped the stem of a tulip at a slant and tucked it into the arrangement. "That's me."

"I'm Adriana Welch. I moved to town from Colorado Springs a couple of years ago."

"Welcome to Bloom, Adriana. What can I help you with?"

"Well, I'm just…having a look around—and this little beauty is Marybeth, right?"

By then Jody had zero doubt that Adriana was after more than a bouquet of flowers. She stuck another tulip in the vase. "How did you know my baby's name?"

Spots of color flamed on Adriana's smooth cheeks. "Well, I know Seth. I met him a few months ago, right after they opened the justice center here in town. I went into the sheriff's office to take care of an overdue speeding ticket, and there he was. He's such a great guy. So steady and kindhearted, with that dry sense of humor…"

So. A card-carrying member of the Seth Yancy fan club. Jody should have guessed. "Did you make the key lime pie? Amazing. Or the double-chocolate cake? Unbelievable. Or wait. How about those deep-dish oatmeal chocolate bars? I have to tell you, at this rate I'll never lose the baby weight."

"I made the cake," Adriana confessed.

Jody groaned just thinking about that cake. "So good. I'll have you know you caused an orgasm in my mouth."

Adriana laughed. "Well, that is the goal." And then she raised a hand and wiggled her fingers. "Sheriff Yancy fangirl—I'll just go ahead and admit it."

Jody felt a little stab of annoyance at this pretty woman who baked a killer chocolate cake and also appeared to be a very nice person. Was it jealousy?

Absolutely not. Jody refused to be jealous of someone just because that someone had a crush on Seth. That would make no sense at all.

Well, not unless Jody wanted Seth for herself.

And she'd already come to the firm conclusion that she did not. The entry bell chimed again. A customer left with the arrangement Marlie had just rung up. Three women came in. Marlie went to help them. Adriana leaned closer and pitched her voice lower. "I know I'm being kind of pushy, but I really have to ask…"

Jody added another iris to the vase. "Go ahead."

"Well, Seth makes no secret of how much your baby means to him. He has pictures of her on his phone, and he's been showing them off." Jody wasn't surprised. He'd been snapping photos all weekend: Marybeth on her play mat, Marybeth in her bouncy chair, Marybeth in her newborn-size purple plastic bathtub. In the bathtub shot, he'd sworn she was smiling. Jody hadn't had the heart to tell him it was probably just gas.

"Yeah." Jody cut a generous length of cobalt blue grosgrain ribbon. "He loves his girl, no doubt about that."

"But is he…?" Adriana paused, apparently in search of just the right words. "I heard he's been staying at your house to help out since the birth?"

Jody nodded as she wrapped the ribbon around the neck of the vase. "He's been terrific. I don't know how I would have managed without him."

"But, um, are you two a couple—and, God, I hope it's not too tacky of me to ask?"

Jody tied the bow and fluffed it. "No. It is not the least tacky." Did she sound sincere? She hoped so. Because it wasn't tacky. It was up-front and honest. Not to mention brave. "And Seth and I are *not* a couple. He's just doing what he can for Nick's daughter."

"He's such a good man." Adriana said it with feeling.

"Oh, yeah." *Not jealous. Uh-uh. No way.* "The best."

"And I ask because, well, you know, Library Celebration Day is Saturday."

"That's right." Between having a baby and running her business at the same time, Jody had forgotten all about the event. "It's an all-day thing in Library Park, right?"

"Right. And in the afternoon, the library association is running a bachelor auction. Several local single guys have volunteered to go on the block, including Seth."

No way did that sound like something Seth would agree to. "If you win, what do you get?"

"A date with the bachelor you outbid everyone else for—and I think I heard your brother Garrett got roped into being auctioned off, too." Garrett was second-oldest of Jody's three full brothers and the only one currently unattached.

And Seth's involvement in such a non-Seth-like activity was starting to make sense now. "Roped into it, huh?"

"Pretty much. Have you *met* the president of the library association? Nobody says no to Caroline Carruthers."

Jody knew Caroline. And Adriana was right about her. "So, bottom line, Seth is on the bachelor auction block Saturday, and you want to bid on him?"

Adriana blushed and beamed. "Oh, yes, I do. And I'm not the only one who'd like to win a night out with Seth—I mean, as long as he's not taken."

Jody had a totally contrary urge to put on her meanest face and order the blonde to back off. But that wouldn't be right. Seth was not hers and never would be.

"Jody?" Adriana prompted hopefully.

And Jody made herself say it. "He's not taken."

"But are you sure?" Adriana didn't look convinced.

"Seth Yancy is a free man," Jody insisted with a firm nod. "Go for it. And good luck."

That night at six thirty, Seth used the key Jody had given him to let himself in. The house smelled of something good for dinner. It was great to be home.

Not home. Jody's house, he sternly corrected himself.

He was kind of having trouble lately remembering that he didn't actually live here, that he was only staying temporarily, until Jody decided it was time for him to go.

He hoped she'd let him stay on indefinitely, but he knew that eventually she would want her privacy and the use of her spare room again. She would send him back to the ranch where the Califanos had everything under control and he had the main house all to himself.

Seth loved that old house. Yancys had been born and raised in it for four generations. But with only him living there, the place echoed with emptiness.

Unlike Jody's house, which smelled like dinner and made a man feel welcome, made him feel as though he was part of a family, after all. And he was. Marybeth was his family. Jody, too, when you came right down to it. She and Marybeth were a package, and he was just fine with that.

"I've got stew ready in the Crock-Pot. Hungry?" she asked when he entered the kitchen and went straight to the sink to wash his hands.

"Yeah. Smells good."

She'd already set the kitchen table. He got himself a beer, and they sat down.

"I talked to my dad today," he said as he smoothed his napkin on his lap and reached for his fork. "He wants to fly out for a visit the first week of June. He can't wait to see Marybeth."

"First week of June would be great."

"He would stay at the ranch. But he's pretty excited about being a grandpa, so you'd better expect to have him underfoot a lot around here."

"I'm looking forward to getting to know him."

"Good, then. I'll tell him."

They both got to work on the stew. Seth was just getting that prickly feeling under his skin that she had something on her mind when she said, "Adriana Welch stopped by Bloom to see me today."

He swallowed the hunk of meat he'd just stuck in his mouth. It went down hard. He had no idea why he felt suddenly on edge. Yes, Adriana was one of his supposed fan club, but what could she possibly say to Jody that could get him in trouble? "She's a nice woman, Adriana."

"Yes, I thought so, too…"

That. Right there. The way her voice trailed off at the end. What did that mean, exactly?

He asked with great caution, "And she came by to see you, why?"

Jody sipped her ice water and set the glass down just so. "She and several other women plan to bid on you at the bachelor auction Saturday."

The bachelor auction. A raw litany of bad words scrolled through his brain. He'd been trying not even to think about Saturday. It was coming up way too fast.

Jody added, "Adriana wanted to check with me first, though, to make sure you're not taken."

"Taken," he repeated blankly. And then he said it again, this time as a question. "Taken?"

"Well, Seth. You've been living in my house for weeks. It's natural that your admirers would start to wonder if you and I are doing more together than looking after the baby."

Seth drank some beer—a big gulp of it, as a matter of fact. "I hope you set her straight," he said. And then as soon as the words were out, he wanted to snatch them back. Because he honestly wouldn't mind in the least if people thought he and Jody were together.

If he and Jody were together, he would never have to go back to living alone. He could be with her and Marybeth, have a permanent place with them. Every day that passed, he wanted that more.

"I told her not to worry, that you definitely weren't taken."

"You encouraged her." It came out sounding like an accusation—which he supposed it was.

"Yes, I did. It's the truth. You're *not* taken. And besides, you want women bidding on you, the higher the better."

"No, I don't."

"Well, you should. It's for a good cause."

"I don't like it, Jody. I never liked it. That Carruthers woman just wouldn't take no for an answer."

"Seth. Come on. It'll be fun."

"No, it won't."

She made a low, teasing sound in her throat. "You know what you sound like?"

"Don't tell me."

But of course, she did. "An overgrown baby. Pull up your big-boy pants and stop with the tantrum."

He gave her the kind of look he usually reserved for repeat offenders. "I am a grown man. Grown men do not have tantrums." She just shook her head and ate more stew. And he couldn't stop himself from asking, "Will you be there?"

She frowned. "For the auction? I wasn't planning to, no."

He wanted that, he realized. He wanted her there. A lot. "It's a whole-day thing. With booths, games, food, music. The auction is from two to four. You could bring Marybeth. You'll have a great time."

Her mouth was twitching. He failed to see what was so all-fired amusing. "Seth, the last thing I need is to bid on a bachelor—and you'd better not be working up to asking me to bid on *you*."

Why not? That sounded like an excellent idea to him. He could give her the money. She could win him, and he wouldn't have to go out with Adriana or some other nice woman he had zero interest in romantically. It wouldn't exactly be fair play. But the library would still get the money, and that was the goal.

However, the way she was looking at him, he knew she wouldn't go for that. So he fibbed, "No way would I ask that of you."

She didn't believe him. He could see it in those fine blue eyes. But she played along. "Good."

"I just need a little moral support from my two favorite girls, that's all. Caroline Carruthers wouldn't take no for an answer, and now I'll be going out with some woman from town, and the truth is, I have a firm rule about that."

"What rule?"

"I don't date local women."

"Why not?"

He didn't want to get into it. But somehow, he found

himself telling her anyway. "Because I know it's never going to go anywhere with anyone, so to date someone in my county is just going to lead to trouble in the end. I don't want things to get messy. I'm the sheriff, after all."

She sat back and folded her arms. Not a good sign. "How 'bout this? Maybe if you took a chance, went out on a limb and spent an evening with a nice woman, you might change your mind and realize you would like to get something going with her, after all."

"I won't. That isn't going to happen."

She put both hands to her head, as though this conversation might possibly cause her brain to explode. "Seth. How can you be so sure?"

"I have no interest in a relationship. I'm the sheriff, and it's on me to set a good example—which means *not* leading innocent women on."

Jody outright scoffed at him then. "Oh, come on. It's the twenty-first century. Not a trembling virgin in sight."

Now he felt kind of insulted. "I wouldn't encourage a virgin—especially not a trembling one."

"Great, then. Because Adriana seems confident and savvy to me. She's not going to expect anything beyond a nice evening out with you if she wins a date with you— and I'm betting the rest of the women who might bid on you are the same, right?"

He didn't want to answer her. He knew it would only get him deeper into this uncomfortable conversation that he didn't want to be having in the first place.

"Right?" she demanded again.

He gave in and said it. "Right."

"So then, I can promise you that none of them will

expect a lifetime commitment because you took them out."

"I just don't believe in any of that."

She looked at him sideways. "Um, any of what?"

"Dating someone when I know it's not going to go anywhere."

Jody sat forward again, picked up her dinner roll, tore it in half and then dropped it back to her plate. "It doesn't have to go anywhere. I mean, come on. You don't have to be married to have a good time with someone."

He opened his mouth to backpedal a little, but ended up blurting out the bald truth about himself instead. "I'm not after a good time with someone. I don't believe in sex outside of marriage—or without love, at least. Preferably both."

Jody gaped. "I don't know where to start. By *a good time*, I don't necessarily mean sex. But as long as we're going there, you've never *been* married. Have you?"

"No, I have not."

Her head went back and forth, and her eyes were wide as dinner plates. "I know I shouldn't ask…"

"No, you probably shouldn't." He drank some beer.

And she asked anyway. "So you've never had sex with anyone?"

He could simply refuse to answer her. But over the past weeks something of a bond had grown between them. He felt a need to make her understand. "I've had sex, yes—with women I wasn't married to. When I was younger I didn't always live up to my beliefs."

She clapped both hands to her mouth, as if trying to keep the next question from getting out.

A hard sigh escaped him. "Go ahead. Ask."

She dropped her hands. "What about Irene, in Chicago?"

He almost just told her to mind her own business. But the bond he felt with her tugged at him. He lived in her house, and he understood that if he wanted to *keep* living there, he needed to make an effort to get along with her, to communicate. "Yes," he said. "Irene and I were lovers. I was in love with her. I'd asked her to marry me and she'd said yes. I already *felt* married to her."

"And after you lost Irene?"

"There's been no one. Except myself, I guess you could say."

"Wait a minute. Not a single date? You didn't meet someone for coffee? Nothing?"

"There were dates, yeah, after I'd been back here in Colorado for a couple of years. I'm human, after all." He watched her sip that weird herbal tea she liked and waited for a teasing remark concerning his humanity or lack thereof. But no. She was quiet, her gaze locked with his over the rim of her mug. So he continued, "I went out with a few women I met online."

"I'm guessing these were women who didn't live in Broomtail County?"

"You're guessing right. I took them to dinner and maybe a movie and then I took them home. But I knew it wasn't going anywhere, that I was kidding myself and wasting their time and mine. I didn't want sex with a stranger. And I didn't want a relationship. So after a while, I stopped looking, online or otherwise."

"How long since you returned to Colorado from Illinois?"

"Seven years."

"Oh, Seth." She said it way too softly. Too...tenderly.

"What?" he demanded in a growl.

"I can't decide if I'm sad for all you've missed out on—or in awe of you for having principles and managing to stick by them for seven long years."

"Awe. I'll take awe."

She laughed. And then he laughed, too, of all things. The sound was pretty rusty. But still, it felt good.

They picked up their forks and started eating again. Neither of them spoke for several minutes.

He scooped up the last bite of his stew. As soon as he'd chewed and swallowed, he took another stab at getting her to be there Saturday. "Please, come to the park for the auction."

She looked up from mangling her dinner roll. "It's not going to be that bad. And it's only one date."

"You sound like Caroline Carruthers," he grumbled. And then he leveled his gaze on her and willed her to give in. "Please, come. I want a friend there."

At 1:45 on Saturday afternoon, Library Park was packed.

People wandered from booth to booth, buying T-shirts, books and library paraphernalia, handmade crafts and art by local painters and photographers. Kids played tag between the trees. There was a food pavilion—a giant white canopy over rows of picnic tables, food carts surrounding the covered tables. Under another wide white canopy beside a portable stage, a six-piece band played country rock.

Jody, in jeans and a Bloom T-shirt, black Chucks and a Broncos hat, pushed Marybeth in her stroller and made a mental note to find out if this would become an annual event. If so, next year, she'd see about getting Bloom involved somehow.

"Darling!"

Jody glanced back and saw her mother, gorgeous as always in black capri pants, an off-the-shoulder lace-work shirt and sexy wedge sandals, coming toward her. "Ma!" She wheeled the stroller under a tree, out of the way of the crowd.

"It's so good to see you." Willow took her by the shoulders and air-kissed her cheek, bringing the scent of sandalwood and tropical flowers, a fragrance that some shop in Paris made just for her. "I flew in this morning, and Estrella said the magic words *party in the park* and *bachelor auction*." Estrella Watson was the Bravo Mansion's longtime housekeeper. "Well, I had to see for myself—and what have we here?" Willow dipped to a graceful crouch beside the stroller. "Hello, beautiful. It's me, your grandmother, who completely adores you." Marybeth was having another good day. She waved her hands at her grandma and cheerfully cooed. "She's perfect. I have a few little treasures for her. I must drop by with them. Soon."

"Anytime. I'm at the shop a few hours a day, but the times vary. Just call my cell first."

"I will." Willow swept upward again. "You look well. A little haggard."

Gee, thanks, Ma. "I keep busy."

"Don't wear yourself to a nub, now."

Jody tried not to grit her teeth. "Ma, I will do my best."

"Excellent. So. Are you here to nab yourself a bachelor?"

"No."

"I hear Caroline Carruthers managed to round up the hottest, most successful single men in town—including your brother Garrett," Willow added with pride.

Jody was stuck back there with her mother talking about hot men. Did Willow plan on bidding? Eww. "Uh, yeah. Garrett's on the block, all right."

"I hope some lovely girl wins him. It's about time he settled down."

"Ma. It's for a good cause, but come on. Nobody's ending up married to Garrett because they 'won' him at the library auction."

"Honestly, Johanna." Willow hit her with her given name though she preferred Jody, and Willow knew it, too. "You have zero romance in your far-too-practical soul."

"You may be right." Romance hadn't exactly been good to her so far.

Willow said, "The bachelors have been all over the park today, chatting up women, introducing themselves." Jody tried not to wince for poor Seth. He would just love wandering the park, instigating teasing conversations with random women. Not. Her mother asked coyly, "So, how many bachelors have you met so far?"

"Marybeth and I just arrived." In order to support Seth, who wouldn't shut up about it until Jody agreed to be there when the bidding started.

"Did you at least check out the list of prospects and their bios on the library website? Your sheriff is included."

"He's hardly *my* sheriff."

"Well, he was there for you, right, the night Marybeth was born?" Before Jody could answer her, Willow whipped out her tablet phone and stuck it in front of

Jody's face. "Look." Handsome male faces scrolled up the screen. A picture of Seth went by. He looked manly and determined, a ray of light glinting off the badge on his uniform shirt. "See anything you particularly like?"

Laughing in spite of herself, Jody slipped her hand under the visor of her cap and covered her eyes. "Ma. Stop. Now."

Willow lowered the phone and heaved a sigh so loud it could be heard over the band wrapping up a cover of Sam Hunt's "Make You Miss Me."

"I worry you'll never find what you're looking for, darling, that's all."

Jody stared into her mother's beautiful sea green eyes and reminded herself that Willow just wanted the best for her. "Thank you. But I have everything I need, and I'm happy. I truly am."

Willow made a show of pressing her lips together. "This is me keeping my mouth shut—and look." She pointed at the stage where Caroline Carruthers had stepped up to the mic. "The auction begins."

Caroline spread her arms wide and announced with enthusiasm, "Welcome, everyone, to our first annual Library Celebration Day!" Jody clapped good and loud with everyone else. And then Caroline launched into a spirited speech, starting with how happy she was to see such a crowd on this beautiful May afternoon. She ran down a list of the latest improvements at the library, encouraging everyone to come often and use all the library's services. She reminded them all about the silent auction just waiting for more bids under a nearby canopy, then announced the total donations so far, mostly from people giving money online. She thanked a few donors and volunteers specifically for their generous and ongoing support.

Then she leaned close to the mic and mock-whispered gleefully, "And, yes, ladies and gentlemen, it's that time at last. Fifteen of Justice Creek's best-looking and most eligible single guys are stepping into the spotlight today, offering fifteen fortunate and generous women the chance for the date of their dreams. I present to you...the bachelors of Justice Creek!"

The band played "Fever," and out they came, most of them good-naturedly strutting, some even busting Magic Mike–like moves. They wore tight jeans, cowboy boots and snug, muscle-showcasing T-shirts printed with library-themed humor: "Reading is sexy" and "Meet me in the stacks" and "I read past my bedtime."

Two of the bachelors were firefighters. They wore yellow helmets and red suspenders. Garrett, who ran Bravo Construction, wore a tool belt. Seth had a badge pinned over his heart as did a guy she recognized from Justice Creek PD. The guy from the police department even had handcuffs clipped to his belt. He was one of the better dancers, and he really got the crowd whooping and cheering.

Seth didn't dance. He walked in and stood at the end of the line of men. And she had to hand it to him. He looked dangerously hot not doing anything, just standing there in jeans that hugged his hard thighs and that tight black T-shirt that clung to his chest like it was in love with him. No wonder the women couldn't quit baking him pies.

Jody knew he was looking for her. She watched those eagle eyes scanning the crowd. She gave him a hint of a nod when he spotted her and felt a certain lovely warmth low in her belly at the way his hard face softened when their gazes met.

Her mother leaned close. "Okay, Johanna. There's more than love for Marybeth going on with you and Seth Yancy."

"Mind your own business, Ma," she replied out of the side of her mouth.

"You know I'm bound to find out anyway."

She would, of course. That Seth spent all his free time at Jody's place was no secret. Jody went ahead and admitted, "He's been helping me out."

"Helping you out, how?"

"You name it, he helps with it. We've become friends, I guess you could say. And since we brought Marybeth home from the hospital, he's been staying at my house nights, in the spare room."

"No." There was far too much breathless glee in that single word.

Jody looked her mother square in the eye. "Yeah."

That silenced Willow—at least for now.

Caroline went down the line, spending a minute or two with each bachelor, getting their names, their ages, their occupations and their interests. Then the men filed offstage, and a couple of guys brought on a podium. A rangy older man in a cowboy hat came on. Caroline introduced him as the auctioneer. He moved behind the podium. The band played "Let's Get It On" and out came the first bachelor.

The bidding began.

It was actually kind of exciting. And a lot of fun. The guy from Justice Creek PD was third to last and brought nine hundred bucks, which had everyone hooting and hollering in glee. Garrett was next. He had that killer smile, and he joked about his tool belt and what good care he took of his tools. A nice bidding war ensued over him. He brought twelve hundred, the best price so far.

And then there was Seth. He strode onstage to "Pour Some Sugar on Me," not even cracking a smile. How did he do it? He walked straight and stood proud and somehow the temperature in the park rose by ten degrees—or was Jody the only one who felt the heat?

Caroline had questions on cue cards from the ladies in the crowd. Seth answered them straight-faced, big arms folded across his powerful chest.

The bidding commenced. A lot of women joined in, Adriana Welch leading the pack. She topped each competing bid.

Seth stood mostly unmoving through the process, wearing his sternest, most sheriff-like expression, not friendly at all, yet somehow so…magnetic. He was like some giant tree that begged to be climbed. Every woman in that park seemed to feel the power of his uncompromising stare. Didn't they?

Jody certainly did.

And he kept looking at her, glances that burned right through her. She knew what he was doing. That man was willing her to save him from Adriana and the rest of them. But Jody stood firm. It wasn't her job to rescue him, and it wasn't going to kill him to spend an evening out with someone like Adriana, someone pretty and fun.

Or so she kept telling herself every time she almost let her hand shoot up to join in the bidding war.

And not because he willed her to, either. Not to save his fine butt from the women who adored him.

Uh-uh. Not to help him out.

But because she wanted to—wanted to place the

winning bid and get all those other girls to back the hell off. Wanted to stake her claim and make sure everyone knew that he belonged to her.

Which he did not. Not in any way.

What was the matter with her? This could be a problem and she knew it. She never should have let him talk her into coming to the park today. She should have stayed home, not let herself get involved in any way.

Jody held her arms down tight to her sides and set her mind firmly on not raising a hand, no matter what. All she had to do was last until the auctioneer banged his gavel on the podium and shouted, *Sold!*

And then her mother leaned close. "Win that man," Willow commanded. "Or I'll do it for you."

Jody sent her mother her best arctic glare. "Ma. Don't you dare."

Willow did dare.

She lifted her shapely arm, snapped her perfectly manicured fingers to get the auctioneer's attention and took the next bid.

Chapter Seven

Adriana countered Willow's bid. Another woman countered that.

And Willow bid again.

A lot of people knew Willow Mooney Bravo. They knew the story of Willow and Frank and Frank's first wife, Sondra. To most longtime residents of Justice Creek, Willow was considered nothing short of a home-wrecking femme fatale.

Jody wanted to sink right through the grass to the center of the earth as all around her and her baby and her infuriating mother, people snickered and stared and a few of them even whispered to each other. They laughed and they clapped. Jody knew what at least a few of them were wondering: Had bad Willow Bravo suddenly decided to put a move on hunky, upstanding Sheriff Yancy? What would she do to him? Something ruinous, wicked and wild, no doubt.

The last to drop out against Willow was Adriana. Willow topped her final bid by shouting, "Fifteen hundred!" It was two hundred dollars higher than Adriana's bid. Everybody clapped.

The auctioneer pounded his gavel and asked Adriana for fifty bucks more. She shook her head. "Going once," warned the auctioneer. "Going twice..."

Seth had relaxed since Willow started bidding—oh, he was still standing there with his arms crossed and his legs braced apart, his expression carved in stone. But after living with the guy for weeks, Jody could read him pretty well. She saw the twitch at the corner of his mouth that gave away his effort not to smile.

Apparently, he'd figured out what her mother was up to, that Willow was set on winning him for Jody. And being won by Jody was what he'd been after all along.

Because they were good buddies, Seth and Jody. Because he could count on her not to try to put a move on him. With Jody, things wouldn't get "messy."

For some reason, that he was so pleased with her mother's machinations annoyed Jody no end. If she was going to win the guy anyway, she would damn well make it happen herself.

Jody stuck up her hand.

The whole park seemed to go absolutely still. Silence echoed in the balmy air.

The auctioneer pointed his gavel at Jody. "Fifteen fifty." He aimed the gavel at her mother. "An even sixteen?" Willow gave a tiny shake of her golden head. The auctioneer scanned the crowd. "Do I hear sixteen? Ladies? Don't miss out! Going once, going twice..." The gavel went down. "Sold to the lady in the Broncos cap for 1,550 dollars!"

The crowd went wild, clapping, laughing, whistling. Throwing their hats in the air.

"Attagirl." Willow patted her shoulder. Jody turned to say something sarcastic, but her mother had already set off through the crowd.

Caroline Carruthers called, "Winners, congratulations! Come on up here and claim your men!"

There was more hooting and hollering. That last burst of sound finally woke Marybeth up. She started to cry.

Jody pushed the fussing baby forward toward the stage. When she got there, Seth could soothe Marybeth. After all, she'd paid fifteen fifty for him. He could at least make himself useful.

Seth was waiting for her, looking way too pleased with the way things had turned out. He jumped down off the stage, took the stroller with Marybeth in it and hoisted it up there. Then he reached for Jody.

She shook her head. "I'll take the stairs."

But he grabbed her by the waist and lifted her anyway.

As her feet left the ground, she clutched his giant shoulders and let out a shriek. "Seth, put me down!"

And he did—on the stage, which brought another loud flurry of applause and laughter from the crowd. Then he jumped right up beside her, grabbed her hand and raised it high. "Smile," he commanded. "Give the folks a wave."

It was done. She'd won the guy. Might as well give the crowd what they wanted. Jody smiled and waved, which caused more clapping and stomping and catcalls.

When Seth finally let go of her hand, he bent right down to Marybeth, lifting her so gently out of the stroller and up to his shoulder. The ripple of applause increased again, but Marybeth didn't seem to care about all the noise now. She snuggled right in.

They joined the other bachelors and their dates. Caroline thanked the crowd and the auctioneer. She congratulated the winners and reminded them of the table under the tree where three library-association ladies waited with open cash boxes and credit-card readers to take the money the winners had bid.

To a final round of applause, the group on the stage disbanded. Seth put Marybeth back in the stroller long enough to get her down off the stage.

Jody jumped down after them. "If you'll take the baby for a minute, I'll settle up with the library ladies."

Marybeth had started fussing the minute he put her back in the stroller, so he scooped her up again and cradled her close. The crying stopped.

"I'll take care of the money," he said. "It's only fair."

Jody made a show of rolling her eyes. "What in the world has fairness got to do with this?"

He leaned closer, and she got a tempting whiff of his manly, clean scent. "Come on, Jody. I know your mom forced your hand. Let me pay for this. I want to."

"Ah, but see, *that* wouldn't be fair." She poked him in the chest with a finger. It was like poking a boulder. "I won you. I'll pay for you."

He shook his big head and patted the baby on his shoulder. "There's no making you see reason when you get that stubborn look."

"It's settled, then. Watch the baby. I'll be right back."

"I'll go with you, at least."

Together, they headed to the long table under the tree. Jody pulled her credit card from her cross-body bag and waited her turn to pay. Seth, at her side, held Marybeth in one arm and pushed the stroller with his free hand, making himself useful as he always did. The guy was way too easy to have around.

Jody tried to keep in mind all the ways he irritated her. Didn't work. Her frustration with the situation had faded to nothing.

Seth was happy and so was Marybeth. It felt great to be out in the sun on a beautiful day. Yeah, he'd just cost her more than fifteen hundred bucks. But hey. It would go to a good cause.

At the front of the line, she offered her credit card to the lady from the library association. "I won the sheriff." Beside her, Seth actually dared to chuckle, and she had to stop herself from poking him in the ribs with an elbow.

But the library lady shook her head. "Your bid's been paid."

"By who?"

The library lady peered at her list. "Mrs. Franklin Bravo."

Ma. She should have known.

Jody turned and glared at Seth, who was actively grinning. Seriously, the man never cracked a smile, but today he couldn't stop smirking. "What are you going to do if my mother wants her date with you?"

His grin vanished. She found his look of bewildered surprise way too gratifying.

But then the library lady piped up with, "Are you Johanna Bravo?"

"Yeah. So?"

"It says here that you are the holder of the winning

bid. Mrs. Bravo has only paid it for you. The date with the sheriff is yours."

Jody whipped her head around to find Seth starting to smirk again. "Wipe that smile off your face," she commanded. He tried to look innocent, but didn't succeed. She turned back to the lady behind the cash box. "As you just pointed out, *I* won the sheriff. I want to pay for my prize."

"I'm so sorry," said the library lady. "But this bid is already paid. It's a donation freely given. We don't refund donations."

Jody tapped her Chuck Taylor. Damn her mother anyway. Willow just *had* to have the last word.

And really, Jody should have been happy with Willow paying up. Her mother had a lot more money than Jody did. Plus, Jody had only won Seth because her mother had manipulated her into it. It could definitely be considered fair that Willow should pay.

Beside her, Seth cleared his throat.

She froze him with a glance. "Shh. I'm thinking." And that was when the solution came to her. She gave the library lady a gracious nod. "All right, then. I'd like to make a donation for 1,550 dollars, please."

As the library lady's eyes lit up, Seth growled, "Jody…"

She shushed him again. Yes, shushing was rude, but she didn't feel like listening to him tell her what to do. "It's tax deductible," she muttered, as if that explained everything. "And it's for a good cause."

"Oh, yes, it is!" chirped the library lady as she accepted Jody's credit card.

Once Jody had signed for the money and received her tax-deductible receipt, her Silver Star Limo voucher and gold-embossed coupon for a full day of pampering at Sweet Harmony Day Spa, Seth suggested, "Why don't we hang around for a while, get something to eat and enjoy the band?"

"Oh, right," Jody scoffed. "Now the auction's over and you don't have to worry about one of your admirers putting a move on you, you're feeling good."

He didn't even pretend to deny it. "Hey. Got me there. Let's get a hot dog."

"Why not?" Marybeth seemed content. If she got hungry, Jody had pumped milk that morning and had a bottle ready to feed her.

They stayed for two hours. Jody devoured a chili dog and a tall lemonade, and they made the rounds of the craft, art and book booths, meeting up with Clara and Dalton and their little girl, Kiera, for a while and later running into Jody's half brother James, his wife, Addie, their seven-month-old, Brandon, and Addie's grandfather and her grandfather's girlfriend, too. They all sat together at a picnic table to catch up.

More than one of the other women who had bid on Seth stopped by to congratulate Jody on her win, Adriana among them. She leaned close to Jody and teased, "We all knew there was more going on with you two than you admitted the other day."

Jody played along. "It was the tight T-shirt. I realized I *had* to have him."

Seth, sitting next to Jody feeding Marybeth her bottle, heard what both women had said.

He knew Jody was joking, but her response pleased him anyway. Somehow he kind of liked the idea of Jody laying claim to him. He liked just about everything right at this moment.

Was this happiness? It sure felt like it.

Seven long years had passed since he last felt this way, felt that the world had more good in it than evil, that today was a fine day and tomorrow would be great, too.

He looked down at the baby he held in his arms. She waved her little fist and made soft smacking noises as she sucked on her bottle. That feeling happened in his chest, a good kind of tightness, a warmth. A rightness. He'd only truly loved a few people in his life: his dad, his stepmother, Nicky and Irene.

And now there was Marybeth. There had been too many losses. But Marybeth made up for a whole lot of loss.

Beside him, Jody laughed at something her brother James had said. Seth liked Jody's laugh. It was low and rich and real. It reached down inside him and stirred things up. At first, he'd fought that stirring. But sometime in the past week or so, he'd given in and let himself be stirred.

He liked a lot of things about Jody. She was smart and beautiful and easy to be around. She didn't take any crap from him, and he admired her for the way she stood up for her beliefs. He'd also grown to respect her. Slowly, he'd come to appreciate her ingrained integrity. Yeah, she'd made some choices he would never have made. But she owned her mistakes, took responsibility for her actions.

He fully understood now why Nicky had fallen for her.

And as for himself? He'd finally faced the truth.

He was attracted to her. He couldn't deny it anymore, didn't want to deny it.

They were compatible, him and Jody. They worked well together. He'd lived in her house for three and a half weeks and their lives just naturally seemed to fit together like the parts of a well-oiled machine. They never argued over household stuff. They both just kept at it till everything that needed doing got done. They picked up the slack for each other.

They were a good team.

And lately, in the past few days anyway, maybe longer, he kept finding himself thinking that they could have a good life together, raise Marybeth together, be a family, even have more kids...

That night, when Jody dropped down beside him on the sofa in the great room after putting Marybeth to bed, he muted the basketball game and asked, "So where do you want to go for our big date?"

She made a sound of amusement low in her throat. "What date? I want you right here doing what you always do, rocking the baby, changing the diapers, bringing the baked goods and the takeout for dinner—and washing up the dishes afterward."

Actually, he loved the sound of that. "Whatever you want from me, Jody, it's yours."

She drew up her bare feet and crossed them on the cushions. "Wow. That was downright affectionate."

He wanted to touch her—that silky brown hair, the curve of her cheek. Yeah, he still loved Irene and that was forever. After losing her, he'd known that he would never get married.

But now there was Marybeth, and she changed how

he looked at things. He and Jody could make a good life together—good for each other, good for Marybeth. "Ever been married?"

She grabbed a throw pillow and bopped him on the shoulder with it. "Really? Suddenly you want to talk about my past relationships?"

He picked up the remote again and turned the game off. "What's wrong with that?"

"I don't know. It just seems...un-Seth-like, somehow. I mean, you're always willing to listen when I need to talk something out, and I appreciate that about you. But you're not exactly one of those guys who *asks* for it."

"Look. I like you."

"Um. I like you, too?"

He almost laughed. She did that to him. Made him want to laugh again. "Do you *really* like me, Jody?"

She hugged the pillow to her chest. "Of course I do."

"Good. Ever been married?"

"Never."

"Serious relationships?"

She hugged the pillow tighter and tipped her head to the side, studying him. "You honestly want to know." That time it wasn't a question.

"Yes, I do."

She tipped her head the other way and stared at him some more. Then, finally, she gave it up. "No, I have never been married. After my father carried on a quarter-century-long affair with my mother while still married to his wife and then my high school boyfriend dumped me because I was having his baby, I had some serious trust issues when it came to men, I guess you might say."

"Understandable."

She put the pillow in her lap and fiddled with the fringe on it. "After I came back from Sacramento, I went to CU for a business degree. And I went a little wild in college. I had more than a few lovers. But there was nobody serious. I wanted things casual. I didn't want to get too close." She slanted him a wary look. "Don't get judgy, now."

He hadn't been judging her. Had he? "What makes you think I'm judging you?"

"I know how you are, Mr. Straight-and-Narrow."

"Jody. Come on. I told you I had some wild years myself."

She laughed then. "Point taken. So, I kept things casual, but I *was* looking."

"For?"

"A good guy, a trustworthy guy. When I was twenty-three, I found that guy. Or so I thought. His name was Brent Saunders. Brent was an insurance adjuster here in town. He was also kind and gentle and thoughtful. I just knew I had found what I was looking for. We were together for four years."

"What went wrong?"

"Brent was never quite ready to talk about marriage. At first, that worked for me. I wanted to take my time, to be sure it was the real thing with him. We'd been together about eight months when he told me he loved me. I said I loved him, too. After that, he was always saying it. But he never said a word about forever. After two years together, I told him my goals, which included marriage and children—marriage to *him*, I hoped."

"So then, he finally proposed?"

"Not a chance. Brent was vague on the marriage thing. He loved me more than his life, he said. But why rush into anything? We had plenty of time. After four years together, I finally admitted to myself that Brent and I were going nowhere. I broke it off. Three months later, he eloped with the receptionist at his office. They moved to Seattle soon after."

"What a jerk. Not to mention, a fool."

"Thank you. I mean, he could've had *me*."

"He was an idiot."

She hugged her pillow again. "You're kind of a hard-ass, Seth."

"Me? No. I'm gentle. Trustworthy. Thoughtful, too."

She snorted a little as she stifled a giggle. "What I meant is that being a hard-ass is only on the outside. Deep down you're a softy. And sometimes you do say just the right things."

"I say what I really think."

"Mostly. Except when you put on your Mount Rushmore face and say nothing at all."

"Sometimes less is more when it comes to talking."

"Said no woman, ever." Her cheeks were pink, and those blue eyes gleamed. And her mouth. He liked the shape of it, the pretty dip of the Cupid's bow on top, the softness below.

He wanted to kiss her. But he held himself in check. For now. "But about Brent…"

She cocked an eyebrow. "Yeah?"

"It must be a relief that you never said yes to that bozo."

"Well, he would've had to ask in order for me to say yes to him, but you're right. It worked out for the best."

"And after Brent the bonehead?"

"Hmm. Brent the bonehead. Catchy. I like it."

"After Brent…?"

"After Brent, I seriously considered swearing off love and romance for good. I was twenty-seven when I broke it off with him. I decided to focus on my business, on my family and friends. It was fine for a couple of years. And then I started feeling that I was missing out on the most important things. I still didn't know if I would ever find *the* one. But I kind of started thinking I needed to get out and try to meet up with guys again. And then, one night last August, I decided to get out and party. I went to Alicia's."

"And you met Nicky…"

"Yes, I met Nick."

"No one since that night with him?"

She met his eyes steady-on. "No one. Somehow, I always get it wrong, romance-wise, and I've kind of made peace with that. I've got Marybeth now. She and I are a family."

He resisted the urge to correct her, to say that he was part of her family, too. He wasn't. Right now, they were connected through Marybeth. Right now, they were friends. As she and Nicky had been.

Seth wanted more. How to get her to give him more, that was the question.

Jody said, "So. Now you know way too much about me. And I still don't really understand what happened in Chicago, how you lost Irene."

Irene. No way did he want to talk about Irene. Ever.

But if he wanted a chance for a future with Jody, he was going to have to answer her questions, lay it out for her, say what had happened and how.

He admitted, "I don't even know where to start."

Jody reached out and touched his shoulder, a little pat of reassurance. He wanted to grab her fingers, pull her toward him, hold on tight and not let go. But then she took her hand back and wrapped it around her pillow. "Tell me about her. Just start with the easy stuff. Was she tall? Petite?"

"Tall," he said. "Irene was tall, with black hair and eyes to match…" His voice deserted him.

Jody helped him out again. "Serious? Playful? Intellectual? Shy?"

"She could talk to anyone. She was outgoing. And happy, a happy person." Something had eased inside him. It wasn't such a hard thing, to talk about her, about the woman who had been everything to him.

"What kind of work did she do?"

"Irene ran a diner called the Olympia. She'd pretty much grown up there, she and her older sister. But by the time I met her, she was running the diner alone. She couldn't stand to see anyone hungry. I used to tease her that she gave away more meals than she sold."

"She was generous."

"Yeah. Generous to a fault. Her mom had died when she was sixteen, and once her mom was gone, her dad started drinking too much. The older sister got married and moved to Kansas City, so Irene took over the diner. Then her dad died, and she was on her own. The Olympia was two blocks from Chicago Lawn Station, where I worked. That's how I met her. I went in for a ham on rye with mustard, and it was love at first sight."

"Really?" Jody was smiling. "You. In love at first sight…"

He offered a shrug, muttered, "What can I tell you?"

"More. Just…more."

"I asked her out."

"And?"

"She said yes. Six months later, I asked her to marry me. She said yes to that, too. I was the happiest man alive. We were planning a June wedding. She gave up her apartment and I gave up mine, and we got a larger one together. I was about to make detective, and life couldn't have been better..."

Jody asked, "Did she ever come to Colorado?"

He shook his head. "No. We kept planning a visit. But somehow, it never quite worked out that we could both get away at the same time." They should have *made* time; he saw that now. Because you never know when you're going to end up out of time.

"And then?" Jody softly prompted.

All of a sudden, his throat felt like he had something stuck in it. He coughed into his hand to loosen the tightness. "It was a Friday morning in April. I was off-duty, and Irene's head waitress was opening the diner for her. It was raining, a sleety, slushy kind of rain. And we were out of coffee. I said I'd make a run to the corner store. She wanted to go with me. So we went together, sharing her umbrella, running through the freezing rain..."

Irene had been laughing, he remembered, when he pulled open the door for her. She had a great laugh, full out and full of life, and there were drops of rain caught in her black hair as she lowered her umbrella.

"Seth?" Jody was waiting.

He got on with it. "There was a guy. A guy in a Dracula mask holding a .38 on the woman behind the counter." A soft gasp escaped Jody. And suddenly, the words were surging in him, pushing to get out. He couldn't get it over with fast enough now. "I saw what was happening as the guy turned and pointed the revolver at Irene. I shouted, 'Down, Irene!' The guy in the mask swung the gun on me, which was exactly what I wanted him to do. I had my service weapon in a shoulder holster under my jacket. It wasn't the greatest neighborhood, and people knew I was with CPD, so I was in the habit of carrying even in civilian clothes. He turned on me and I went for my weapon, knowing I would probably take a hit, but with a minimum of luck I could get in a good shot even if I went down. But Irene. Irene didn't get down. She cried out, 'No!' and she threw herself in front of me."

Jody made a strangled sound. And once again, the words had backed up in his throat.

He had to force himself to finish it. "The shot stopped her heart. She died giving me just enough time to pull my weapon and kill that sucker as the woman behind the counter pulled hers and shot him, too."

"Oh, Seth." Jody clutched her pillow, eyes wet and glittering, tear tracks down her cheeks.

"She was…everything. My life." The words sliced like razor blades in his throat.

It made him furious. Furious and sick at heart, to remember. Looking back, he could see all those separate moments that had led to her death. All the seemingly meaningless decisions that he might have made differently. If he'd bought coffee the night before. If he'd insisted on going to the corner store alone. If he'd entered the store first, if he'd pushed her down instead of *telling* her to get down.

Jody was watching him. And she knew him well enough now to get where his mind was tracking. "It wasn't your fault. Objectively, you know that. Right?"

"It doesn't matter."

"That's a lie. Come here."

He regarded her warily. "Why?"

"Because I want to hug you. I want to grab you and hold you and tell you it will be all right."

What possible good could a hug do? "But it's not all right."

"I can see that." She just kept watching him from her end of the couch.

And then he was moving, scooting her way, not even knowing he would go to her until he was halfway there. She held out her arms, and he went into them, into her softness, into the scent of her light, fresh perfume and a hint of vanilla from the baby lotion. Twining those slim arms around his neck, she guided his head down into the crook of her shoulder.

It felt good there, in her arms. It felt right. She stroked her fingers through his short hair. He let out a long breath and gathered her closer.

What was it about her? The feel of her body drained the tension right out of him. He could hold her forever.

Hold her, and more.

She stirred him, always had, he realized now. It was partly that cool way she looked at a man, that stubborn streak that rubbed him all wrong at the same time as it excited him. From the first time he noticed her, late last summer when she and Nicky became friends, he'd felt the pull toward her.

And resented it powerfully.

Now he didn't have to resent his desire for her. Now he had plans for her and for him and for Marybeth's future. Now it was only fitting, only right, that he should want this contrary woman.

But then she framed his face between her soft hands and made him look at her. "I'm not buying your crap,

Seth." She gazed way too deeply into his eyes. "It does matter that you know Irene's death wasn't your fault. If you blame yourself, you need to stop. Blaming yourself for something you didn't do is really bad for you, for your spirit. For your heart. For your soul."

How did she do it? The woman could stir his anger as easily as soothe him. He took her by the waist and pushed himself back from her, retreating to his end of the couch, where he glared at her and she stared right back at him, refusing to let him intimidate her.

Finally, he gave it up. "All right. It wasn't my fault. Happy now?" It was a taunt, pure and simple.

But Jody refused to be baited. "After a story like that, it would be pretty hard to feel happy. But I'm glad you told me. You've let me know you a little better, and that's good." She caught her plump lower lip between her teeth, and her eyes were deep as oceans. "Seth, I hate that you lost her. I really do."

He didn't need anyone's pity—nor did he deserve it. "I didn't protect her."

"Keep talking like that." Her voice had gone flat. "I'll hit you with my pillow again."

"It's a fact. I didn't."

She puffed out her cheeks with a hard breath. "On second thought, I won't hit you. I don't need to. You're doing a great job of beating yourself up all on your own."

Okay, so she had a point. There was nothing to be gained by getting bogged down in placing blame and should-have-beens. "Let me try again. I do know it wasn't my fault. But that doesn't change the fact that Irene died for me, and I'm not okay with that. I'll never be okay with that."

* * *

Later that night, sitting in her comfy recliner by the window nursing her baby, Jody couldn't help dwelling on what Seth had told her.

She'd wanted to know what had happened to Irene. Now she did. It didn't feel all that great to know, actually.

But it did help her to understand Seth better. She ached for what he'd suffered. And he couldn't hide the fact that he wasn't over his lost love yet—that Irene still owned his heart.

Jody had to watch herself with him. She really needed *not* to go getting ideas about the two of them getting closer.

He'd loved one woman, loved her completely. And he hadn't been with anyone since that awful rainy morning in Chicago. He wasn't going to suddenly decide to try again just because Jody might have foolishly developed a crush on him.

They were friends. Friends united in the shared goal of giving Marybeth the best that life had to offer. Friends and only friends.

She wouldn't go getting her hopes up that there might be more.

Monday night at dinner, Seth said, "I got us a table at Mirabelle's for seven Saturday night. Why don't you call and set up your day at the spa for Saturday? And give me the limo voucher. I'll call them and reserve a car for Saturday night."

"Mirabelle's?" It was a new restaurant in town, a small, cozy place with white tablecloths and crystal chandeliers and a chef from New York. Everyone said the food was really good and the service impeccable.

"I heard it was good," he said. "Would you rather go somewhere else?"

"I just didn't know we were doing that."

"Doing what?"

"Going through with the date."

He set down his fork. "We're doing it." His voice was deep and rough, and his velvet-brown gaze caught hers and held it.

It just wasn't fair that the guy was so damn hot. *Not happening*, she reminded herself. *Don't get ideas.* "What about Marybeth?"

"It's only a few hours. Get a sitter. Maybe one of your sisters or maybe your mom?"

"Ma? Please."

"She did raise five children, didn't she?"

"She's probably off on her next cruise already."

"A babysitter, Jody. I'm sure you can find one."

"But Marybeth is barely four weeks old."

"Jody. We're going. Stop making excuses."

"And a day at the spa, too? I don't have time for that."

He ate two bites of his pork chop before he spoke again. "I'll look after Marybeth while you're at the spa. But get a babysitter for Saturday night or I'll get one for you. We're going to Mirabelle's."

She sagged back in her chair. "Why are you so determined about this?"

"Because I want to take you out."

"But…you don't go out, remember? There's no point because it can't go anywhere. Not to mention, I live in Broomtail County, and what if it got messy with me?"

"Too late." He was almost smiling. She could see that

increasingly familiar twitch at the corner of his mouth. "It's already messy with you."

"I am not joking, Seth."

"Neither am I. I want to be with you, Jody. And not just as a friend."

"B-but I…" God. She was sputtering. And why did she suddenly feel light as a breath of air, as if she was floating on moonbeams? "You want to *be* with me? But you don't do that. You've made that very clear."

"You're right. I *didn't* do that. Until now. But things have changed."

"Because of Marybeth, you mean?"

"Yeah, because of Marybeth. And because of you, too. Because of the way you are. Strong and honest and smart and so pretty. Because we've got something going on, you and me. Something good. I'm through pretending that we're friends and nothing more. Are you telling me I'm the only one who feels that way?"

"I just…" Her pulse raced and her cheeks felt too hot. She'd promised herself that nothing like this would happen, that she wouldn't get her hopes up.

She needed to be careful. She could end up with her heart in pieces all over again.

"Jody, please go out with me Saturday." He gazed across the table at her, so solid and manly and *real*. The guy who had come for her when she needed him, the man who'd had her back ever since the night her baby was born.

"I…" Where were the words? She had no words.

He pushed back his chair and came around the table toward her. When he reached her side, he held down his hand.

Her heart had come all undone somehow. It bounced

around in her chest like a rabbit on steroids. She put her hand in his. His big, hot fingers closed around her cool ones.

And then he was pulling her up out of the chair. Her napkin drifted to the floor. She made no effort to catch it.

He caught her face between his hands, the hands that had held hers when she was in labor, the hands that could always soothe Marybeth. She stared up at him, mesmerized, as his mouth came down to hers.

His lips were soft. So warm. They felt like heaven on hers, brushing back and forth.

And then settling. Claiming.

She opened on a sigh and let the kiss deepen. His fingers trailed up to her temples, fingertips gently stroking into her hair.

This. Oh, dear, sweet heaven. This.

This was magic. So beautiful and right. And she wanted more of it. More of *him*. She'd taken two big chances in love and both times she'd lost out.

But didn't they all say that the third time's the charm?

What about Irene? warned that wary voice in her head. *He's still not over her.*

Maybe not. Maybe he would never get over Irene. Anything could happen. It could all go so wrong.

But what if this time, it went right instead?

She would never know what she might have had if she didn't take a chance.

"Jody…" He breathed her name against her mouth. "Say you'll go out with me."

She wanted to. So much.

And really, why not?

Right now, at this moment, all he'd really asked for

was that night out she'd won at the bachelor auction. One evening with just the two of them, no dirty diapers, no crying baby to distract them from each other. She didn't have to make a big deal about it. She could just say she would go out with him, take things one step at a time.

He took the kiss deep again, deeper than before. She opened and let him all the way in. His arms came around her, pressing her closer, flattening her breasts against the hard slab of his chest. The scent of him swam around her, so delicious, so right. His tongue explored the secret places beyond her parted lips.

He made her feel cherished. And desired. He...why, he *wanted* her. He really did. The way he kissed her left no doubt on that score. Against her belly, she could feel his arousal. There was heat, real heat, between them. Heat and hunger, too.

How long had it been for her, since a kiss felt this good?

Too long, definitely.

And beyond the building heat, there was the rest of it. The rest of *them*, of Jody and Seth, together. Because they were partners, she realized. And had been for a while now.

Whatever happened in the future, their bond had been established in the birthing suite at Justice Creek General. And it had only grown stronger with every day that passed.

You never knew how things would turn out. You could go to the corner store for coffee and lose it all.

So as long as she was breathing, with strength in her body and hope in her heart, a woman needed to explore all the possibilities.

He lifted his head and his eyes met hers. "Please, Jody. Come out with me."

"All right," she said. "Mirabelle's. Saturday night."

Chapter Eight

Clara agreed to watch Marybeth that Saturday night. She came nice and early and listened attentively to each and every one of Jody's detailed instructions concerning baby care.

Jody knew she was overdoing it. Clara had a two-year-old of her own. She'd changed a thousand diapers and heated up more than one bottle of breast milk. Still, it was Marybeth's first time with a sitter and the first time Jody had left her for an evening. Clara seemed to understand that Jody needed to tell her a bunch of stuff she already knew.

At a quarter of seven, Seth herded Jody out the door toward the limo waiting at the curb. Clara stood in the doorway waving goodbye, a perfectly content Marybeth cradled in her arms.

Mirabelle's, on Grandview Drive, was exactly as

advertised, intimate and so pretty, each table a little oasis of candlelight. The glassware sparkled, the silver gleamed, and a single, perfect orchid on a delicate stem grew from a tiny green ceramic pot. It was still daylight when they got there. Their table had a view of the pale moon suspended above the mountains. The moon glowed brighter as the sky darkened.

Jody had a glass of white wine in honor of the occasion, and they shared an appetizer of poached shrimp with avocado, cilantro and lime. Seth looked way too handsome in his crisp white shirt and gray jacket.

He said, "I like that red dress."

It was simply cut, sleeveless and formfitting. "I was lucky I managed to get it zipped up."

The gold streaks in his eye glowed warmer than ever. "You only had to ask. I would've helped."

Her breath got all tangled up in her throat, and she felt the blush as it colored her cheeks. "You really are flirting with me, aren't you?"

He leaned closer. The light from the antique chandelier overhead cast his eyes into shadow. "You want me to stop?"

It seemed a bad idea to be too truthful. But she did it anyway. "No. No, I don't want you to stop."

He raised his glass of very old whiskey. She tapped it with her wineglass.

The waiter came back a little while later. They ordered salads and entrées. It was all delicious. He wanted to know about her spa day. She said she'd had everything—hair, nails, hot rock massage. She didn't mention the full-out Brazilian. They were only at the flirting stage, after all, and she hadn't been freed up for sex from her doctor yet, anyway. At this point, her going Hollywood was definitely TMI.

However, that she even teased herself with the thought of mentioning it over dinner said a lot more about where this thing with him was going than she was strictly comfortable admitting to herself.

In so many ways he was so rigid, so...traditional. Would he be that way in bed, too? Stiff in a bad way.

She grinned to herself at her little private joke.

And he was watching. "Tell me?"

She shook her head slowly. He had the grace not to push.

When the waiter offered dessert, Jody shook her head. "This dress is tight enough as it is, thank you."

But Seth ordered the chocolate mousse cake anyway and then insisted she have a bite. Or three.

"Will you ride out to the ranch with me?" he asked as they crossed the dark parking lot toward the waiting limousine.

She realized that she wanted to go with him out to the Bar-Y. She wanted it a lot, which kind of surprised her. It wasn't as if she'd never been there before.

Mentally, she calculated how much time she had. They'd spent an hour and a half over dinner, so she had three and a half hours left, max, before she would have to nurse or pump again. So there was time. And Clara should be okay with it. Her sister had urged her to stay out for as long as she wanted; Dalton was looking after their little girl, Kiera, and expected Clara to be gone late.

"I'll have you back with Marybeth by eleven," he promised.

She had her arm in his, and she leaned a little closer to him, into all that heat and strength. "Sure. I'd like to go out to the ranch."

The ride to the Bar-Y took under twenty minutes. It was almost full dark by the time they arrived.

Someone had turned on the porch light of the main house. As the limo rolled to a stop in the light's golden glow, a black Lab ran across the yard from the foreman's cottage. The dog sat obediently by the rear door until the driver pulled it open and Jody got out.

"His name's Toby," said Seth, coming around from the other side of the limo as she bent to pet the dog. "But it looks like you and Toby have already met."

"Once or twice." She let Toby swipe a few kisses on her chin as Seth told the driver what time to come back for them.

The limo sailed off back down the driveway, and Roman Califano, tall, white-haired and whipcord lean, in faded Wranglers and a worn chambray shirt, came out the front door of the cottage. "Seth!" He waved.

Seth waved back and Roman started for them, so Jody and Seth met him in the middle of the yard. She greeted Roman.

He gave her his shy smile. "Good to see you, Jody."

Seth said, "Dad'll be here Monday."

"We're looking forward to it. Mae'll fix his room up nice and make sure the fridge is full." Roman congratulated Jody on her baby and added, "Don't be a stranger. You bring that little one out to meet Mae soon, you hear me?"

"I promise," she said.

With Toby at his heels, Roman headed back to his

place. Seth led Jody up the steps of the two-story ranch house.

Inside, it was as she remembered, the rooms large, the furniture of good quality, but worn. The formal dining room and living room flanked the entry from which stairs led up to the bedrooms on the second floor.

"Nicky ever show you around the upstairs?" he asked.

She shook her head. "We always hung out down here."

"Come on. I'll give you the tour. All this will be Marybeth's someday. You might as well have a look at what belongs to your little girl." He started up the stairs.

Jody was too stunned to move. "You're not serious."

He stopped three steps up and faced her again. "What? You don't want to see the second floor?"

"No—I mean, yes, I do want to see the upstairs. But...you're leaving the ranch to Marybeth? Seriously?"

"Who else would we leave it to?"

"I, well, I just had no idea, that's all."

Looking down from the third step, his hand on the polished wood banister, he studied her face. "Sorry. I guess I just assumed you knew."

"Um, no. I had no clue. I, well... It's wonderful. Thank you—I mean, on behalf of Marybeth."

"Nothing to thank me for." He ran his palm downward along the banister and then back up, as though enjoying the smooth surface of the polished wood. "My father already turned the place over to Nick and me equally back when he moved to Florida, so as of now, with Nick gone, half of the Bar-Y is already Marybeth's. When I go, Marybeth will be the sole Yancy heir. My father's completely on board with that. It's what Nick would have wanted, and it's what I want, too—and you're looking at me like I just sprouted horns and possibly a forked tail."

She laughed at that, the sound a little tight, uncomfortable to her own ears. "It's a surprise, that's all."

He came back down to stand with her at the foot of the stairs. "I suppose you want to know what, exactly, your daughter will be inheriting."

She stared up at him and realized she was happy in that moment, glad that he'd insisted they should have their night out. "Yes. I would love to hear all about the Bar-Y."

He launched into the particulars, his voice rich with pride. "The Bar-Y is 3,500 acres. We've got 1,530 cow-calf pairs, fifty other cows and eleven bulls. We have six horses right now, quarter horses, mostly. There's the ranch house, the bunkhouse, the foreman's cottage, plus a number of outbuildings in good repair and several corrals. We maintain our equipment and our roads. We also own water rights, irrigation systems and 112 miles of fence."

"Well," she said, for lack of anything better. "Marybeth will be so pleased."

He gazed at her steadily, his expression thoughtful now. "Kind of sprung it on you, huh?"

"Yeah. But I'll manage to get over the shock somehow."

"You're not upset with me?"

"For what? My daughter's the heir to a working ranch. It's a lot to take in, but in a very good way."

There was a moment. They gazed at each other. She had the strangest sense that she belonged right here. In this house. With this man.

"The upstairs?" he asked.

She put away her crazy fantasy and replied, "Absolutely. Can't wait to see it."

Up the stairs they went. He showed her the rooms. The master had a walk-in closet, a good-size bathroom and big windows looking out over the backyard. The three other bedrooms shared the hall bath, which was bigger than the master bath, with subway tiles running halfway up the walls and a gorgeous old claw-foot tub.

Downstairs, he took her back through the family room and into the kitchen, where he pulled open the door of the old white fridge. "I have apple juice, Dr Pepper and beer."

"Water?" she asked, her throat gone suddenly scratchy, her eyes burning a little as she thought of Nick, of the first time she'd stopped by to visit him here. He'd offered her the same choices: juice, pop or beer.

Seth shut the refrigerator door and turned to her. He saw her face, and his mouth tipped down in concern. "What is it? What'd I do now?"

"Nothing. You've been wonderful." She bit her trembling lip. "It's just… I haven't been here since a couple of days before Nick died."

His craggy face softened. "It's hard sometimes, huh?"

"Mmm-hmm. And a lot harder for you than for me, I'm guessing."

A floor plank creaked once, a strangely lonely sound, as he closed the distance between them. He put his hands on her shoulders. Her breath caught at the contact. "I'm glad you were with him, that you were his friend. It used to make me mad, that he was so crazy about you and you didn't feel the same."

"I noticed that—and *used to*, meaning you don't feel that way anymore?"

His gaze held hers, steady. Sure. "Now *I* want you. And I'm a guy. A possessive guy. I like it better if I don't have to deal with the possibility that you're still carrying a torch for my brother."

Now I *want you...*

She stared up at him, not sure how she felt. Was this thing with him moving too fast? Probably. Confusion tangled her thoughts. She should tell him to back off. But what she *should* do and what her heart and body yearned for were two completely different things. "I'm not in love with Nick." It came out slightly breathless. "I never was."

"I know. You made that painfully clear that first day I cornered you at your flower shop. And as of now, well, even if you were in love with Nicky, I would get past it."

She wasn't following, exactly. "Past it?"

"I would learn to deal with it if I had to, if you *had* loved Nicky that way—even if you still loved him, I would accept that. I would get over it and move on." His hands glided inward, until his rough palms rested in the twin curves where her neck met her shoulders. A rush of heat blew through her, settling low. "Because I think we could be good together, you and me." His thumbs caressed her, burning twin paths of sensation on either side of her throat.

His brushing touch felt so good. She had to swallow a moan—and then he swooped close and kissed her, a long kiss, slow and deep. Her knees went to jelly. She was lucky she didn't melt to the floor.

By the time he came up for air, all she could do was

gape at him, stunned. And then she made herself ask, "What about Irene?"

He answered without pause, his voice rough as a stretch of bad road. "Irene is gone. Same as Nicky's gone. Deal with it."

"It's not the same. You just said it yourself. I was never in love with Nick. I haven't spent seven years not even letting myself look at another man."

His hand moved down her arm in a slow caress. He caught her fingers. "Let's go outside."

"You're changing the subject."

"That's not necessarily a bad thing."

Was he right? Was she making a big deal out of nothing? She didn't think so. But...

She pulled her hand from his.

His amber gaze turned pleading. "Jody. Don't say no without hearing me out."

"I don't remember there being a question."

"I'm getting there."

She closed her eyes, swallowed. Her mouth and throat were dry as dust. "Water. Please."

He seemed to shake himself. "Yeah. All right." He took a glass from a cupboard and filled it from a pitcher of ice water in the fridge. She drank it down. "More?"

"No, thanks. That'll do it."

He took the glass and put it on the counter by the sink. She watched him move around the empty kitchen, and a strange calm settled over her.

She wanted him, too. She wanted him with her, wanted him at her side, helping her raise her daughter, his niece—and his heir, of all impossible things. She wanted him in the living room at night, waiting for her on the couch while she put Marybeth down to sleep.

She wanted him across the table from her in the morning. And at night for dinner, the two of them sharing the events of their separate days.

And while she was adding up all she wanted from him, she might as well be honest with herself. She wanted him in her bed, too. She wanted him in all the ways a woman can want a man.

And she wanted him more than she'd ever wanted any man before.

Was this love, then? Had love found her for real at last?

Of course not. Talk about getting ahead of herself. And what did she know about real love, anyway?

She'd thought she'd loved Dean, the high school sweetheart who walked out on her. And Brent, who married someone else as soon as they broke up. She'd been so wrong. On both counts.

"Outside?" Seth's hand brushed hers again.

She realized she wanted that, the feel of his hand around hers, encompassing. Undeniable. She accepted his touch, weaving their fingers together that time.

"This way." He took her out the glass doors in the family room, down the back steps to the unfenced backyard, pulling her onward beneath the brightening stars, across the open space, into the trees. It wasn't long before the trees gave way to a clearing, where the crescent of moon shone down and the stars were a million pinpricks in the dark fabric of the night.

A large, flat-topped boulder poked up from the tall, silvery grass in the center of the treeless space. Seth led her to it and pulled her down beside him.

"It's a pretty spot," she said. Beyond the tops of the surrounding trees, in the far distance, the mountains reached for the moon. Everything was silvered in star-light.

"It's *my* spot, my secret place, the place I used to come to be alone. To think. To plan my life. To get over the hard things."

"Hard things like...?"

He turned her hand over and idly traced the lines of her palm with his index finger, his touch warm, gentle. Right. "My mom left when I was still in diapers, ran off with some drifter who came through looking for work. My dad used to tell me that she would come back. She never did. For years after that, until my dad met Dar-lene, he was a distant man. He took care of business, went through the motions of living, but something was missing. The sadness in him went clear to the bone."

"You were lonely as a boy," she whispered.

"Yeah." He gave her hand a squeeze. "I was five or six when I wandered out here for the first time. From then on, I spent a lot of time here, sitting on this rock." He tipped his head back and stared up at the stars. "Until I was ten or so, when I came here I would wish for my mom to come home like my dad kept promis-ing she would. And then I heard the hands talking one day, about how my dad wouldn't give up waiting for a woman who was never coming back. I finally accepted that the hands had it right. By then, I just wanted to get away, be a lawman, fight for right and justice." He chuckled, a sound without much humor in it. "I didn't know how I would do that, exactly. My dad expected me to follow in his footsteps. Being the only Yancy after him, it was my duty eventually to run the Bar-Y. But then along came my stepmom, and my dad was happy again. Plus, there was Nicky, a Yancy to run the ranch…"

"So you got to go live your dream, after all."

He raised his hand, palm out. She pressed hers against it, palm to palm. A delicious shiver traveled up the inside of her arm, into her chest and straight to her heart.

"I'm talking too much," he said.

She slipped her fingers between his and held on. "No, you're not. I like it, sitting here on your special rock in your secret place, learning more about you."

He shifted then. Moving with surprising grace for such a big man and still holding her hand, he slid off the rock and sank to his knees in front of her.

Jody blinked down at him. There was only one reason she could think of for him to take a knee. "What's going on, Seth?"

"I want you, Jody."

Omigod. Had she had any idea he would do this? No. Not a clue. She needed to slow him down. "Seth, I don't think—"

"Wait. Let me finish."

She almost objected again. But then she didn't.

Because deep in her wild and still-hopeful heart, she *wanted* him to finish.

"I want everything with you," he said. Her heart pounded so hard, and her blood raced through her veins. She thought she would faint.

But she didn't faint.

And he had more to say. "I want to take care of you, make things good for you, help you raise Marybeth."

A sound escaped her, not a word, more of an audible sigh.

And he kept on. "I've been so sure for so long that I would never have a family of my own. But I was wrong. You did that, Jody. You and Marybeth. You gave me hope again. You gave me something so good to come home to at night. I'm like my dad—I get that. I need family or I'm dead inside. And you, Jody, you and Marybeth, you are my family. I want to marry you, Jody. I want the world to know that you're mine and I'm yours."

Oh, how did he do that? How did he know to say such beautiful things?

And he wasn't finished yet. "And I'm hoping, maybe, in a few years, if you're willing and it works out that way, there could be more children. I would like that, if we had more kids. But don't get me wrong. If it's only the three of us, that's okay with me. You and Marybeth, you're plenty. You're all that I need." He reached into the inside pocket of his jacket, and when he pulled his hand out, she saw he had a ring, a gorgeous vintage oval-shaped diamond with smaller diamonds glittering on the white gold band. "It was my stepmother's." His eyes shone so bright in the moonlight. "I...hope it's okay."

Jody gasped. "Seth. It's beautiful."

"Say yes to me, Jody."

The absolutely crazy, insane truth was that she wanted to say yes. She *longed* to say yes.

Still, she tried to hold on to her scattered wits, to carefully examine the exact words he had said. The word *love* had not been among them. She knew why, too. He'd *had* love, true, lasting love, and that wasn't what he offered her.

He was, however, offering her forever. A real commitment. He wanted a life with her, just as she wanted one with him.

He was no Dean. He was nothing like Brent. And he wasn't dear, sweet Nick, either. Nick had been wrong for her, too innocent, too young.

But Seth?

Seth was so exactly right. With his rough edges and his bossy ways, his deep need to protect, his limitless tenderness with her little girl.

His unswerving devotion.

Seth understood her. She'd told him her sins and the secret of her lost little boy. He saw the whole of her.

He *wanted* the whole of her.

Forever. She could have that with him. It wasn't perfect. But what in life ever was?

The moon bathed his upturned face in silver. "Jody. Dear God. Say something, please."

"I…" It was all she could manage. There was more, so much more she should be saying. But somehow, her thoughts refused to organize themselves into actual sentences.

"Damn it, Jody." The mild swearword shocked her. Seth never cursed. And then he was rising, sweeping to his feet, pulling her up and into his hard arms, yanking her good and close. "Say yes." His head swooped down. He took her lips in a searing kiss that left absolutely no doubt about the chemistry between them.

Heat sang beneath her skin. She wanted to pull him down in the silvery grass, rip off all his clothes and hers, as well, to lay claim to his big body, right here and now, make him hers in the most fundamental way. So he would know that even if he had to save his heart for the woman who'd died so he would live, she, Jody, owned the rest of him. His body was hers.

But then he lifted his head, and she was gazing up into his shadowed eyes. "Say yes to me, Jody."

He was the man she wanted. And *he* wanted *her*. He wanted to be with her, to take care of her little girl.

They had a true and powerful bond, even if neither of them was willing to call it love.

It was just so right with him, so good. With him, she had everything she'd given up hope of ever finding with a man. And if he saved his words of love for the woman he'd lost so tragically, well, it wasn't as if that woman would ever return to take him back.

"Jody?" He sounded worried now.

And wait.

Hold on a minute.

Really, she needed *not* to get carried away. She should slow this down, take more time. They didn't have to rush into forever. Forever would be waiting for them when they were ready.

But then again, she longed to say yes to him. It burned inside her, the need to accept what he offered her. They were so good together. And she wanted what he wanted, a life together—the two of them and Marybeth. She wanted to live the little fantasy she'd had back there in the front hall of the ranch house, in that moment before he led her up the stairs.

And words of love or not, now that he'd made what he wanted clear and it turned out to be exactly what she wanted, well, her answer really wasn't going to change, was it?

"Say yes," he whispered, prayerfully now.

That did it. She simply could not deny him. Couldn't deny her own hungry heart.

She reached up her left hand and laid her fingers along the side of his face. "Yes."

He made a low sound, desperate and tight. "What was that you said?"

"I said yes, Seth."

He grabbed her hand, pressed a kiss to her fingertips and then slipped that beautiful diamond ring on her finger. "Yes." He kissed her fingers again, breathing the word against her skin. "You just said yes."

She laughed then—at the wonder in his voice, at the look of joy and surprise on his face. "Yes, I did. Let's get married as soon as possible."

And he picked her up and spun her around, right there in the silvery starlight, in the center of the beautiful clearing he'd considered his secret place when he was a boy.

Chapter Nine

They were married right there at the Bar-Y a week later.

Seth's dad, Bill, holding Marybeth in his arms, stood up as Seth's best man. Jody had no attendants, but her sisters were there, her mother and her brothers, too. Once you added in wives, husbands, fiancés, children, employees and various other friends and associates, it was a pretty good-size group for such short notice.

There were plenty of flowers from Jody's shop, and Elise and her crew provided most of the food—but not the wedding cake. For that, Adriana Welch had outdone herself, baking three triple-decker chocolate cakes at Jody's request.

Pastor Jacobs from Elk Street Community Church officiated. Jody wore a retro tea-length blush-pink dress with a fitted bodice and a full skirt, which she'd bought at the local bridal shop, Wedding Belles. She carried a bouquet of bright pink peonies. Her hair was piled up loosely under a short veil.

Elise stepped up and took her bouquet for the vows. A few minutes later, Seth slipped the wedding band that matched her gorgeous engagement ring on her finger.

The minister said, "Seth, you may kiss your bride," and her new husband lifted her veil. Then he cradled her face in his big hands and pressed his warm, soft lips to hers. He kissed her slowly, taking his sweet time about it.

Friends and family pressed in close, but Jody forgot all about them.

There was only the two of them, Jody and Seth, married. Sharing their first kiss as husband and wife. He let his wonderful hands stray down to her shoulders and lower, gathering her close to him, wrapping his arms around her nice and tight as he went on kissing her. She could have stood there in her pink dress with her mouth fused to his into the next century and beyond.

But then Marybeth, in her grandpa's arms, let out a high trill of sound that could have passed for a laugh.

The baby's seeming mirth was contagious. Someone giggled. And then someone else chuckled.

Against her lips, Seth whispered, "More on this later."

And then she was laughing, too.

Pastor Jacobs presented them as Mr. and Mrs. Yancy, and it was official.

She'd married Seth Yancy.

The party lasted until long after dark. When all the guests had finally headed home, Elise's crew stayed to clean everything up. Seth, Marybeth and Jody returned to her house in town. Bill was staying at the ranch house, and Jody and Seth wanted privacy for their wedding night.

The ride back to town was a quiet one. Marybeth snoozed in her car seat. Jody stared out the windshield at the clear, starry June night and tried to ignore the fluttery sensations in her stomach and her ongoing state of near-breathlessness.

She'd been to see Dr. Kapur on Thursday. It was full speed ahead in terms of her sex life with her new husband. She'd had a contraceptive shot that was already working, and she and Seth had discussed protection. Due to their mutual long-term abstinence, they'd agreed that no condoms would be necessary tonight.

It kind of amazed her that she would now have a sex life again after so long. There had only been Nick, that one time, in four years.

And what about Seth? In terms of abstinence, he put her to shame. She slid him a glance. In the dashboard light, he looked so stern and composed.

He must have felt her gaze on him. "What? Say it."

She gulped. Hard. "Just thinking..."

"About sex, you mean?"

A wild, nervous laugh tried to burst out of her. She held it back, but it got away from her and came out as a goofy, snorting sound.

He nodded. "Yeah. I can't wait, either." And then he reached across, took her hand and kissed the back of it. "You're beautiful. And I'm the luckiest guy in the world to be married to you."

At the house, Jody left Seth in the great room with Marybeth.

"I'll be right back," she promised. "I'm just going to change out of this dress."

Just like that, she was gone. He patted Marybeth's tiny back and kissed her temple and thought about how he'd wanted to be the one to take that dress off of his bride. But Marybeth was hungry now, and that made her fussy. It was his job to keep her happy while Jody put on something more nursing-friendly.

"I'll take her now." Jody emerged from the bedroom hallway wearing a loose-fitting blue robe. She took the baby from him and disappeared back down the hallway.

He went to the kitchen, where he got down the whiskey and poured himself a stiff shot. Knocking it back in one go, he put the shot glass down hard. Then he wandered over to the breakfast nook and stood staring blankly at his own shadowed reflection in the window that looked out over the dark backyard.

Married. To Jody. He could hardly believe she'd said yes, given him permission to be with her. To be a father to Marybeth. Now he would never have to move out and leave them.

He would have it all, after all, though he'd long ago given up the last hope of such a thing. He wanted his new wife. Wanted her bad. Wanted her way outside the scope of the boundaries he'd set on himself since the loss of Irene.

And by some miracle, by a chain of impossible events that included not only the birth of his niece but also the loss of his only brother way too soon, he would have her, have Jody. She belonged to him now. As did Marybeth. No one and nothing could take them away from him.

Except death, which came for everyone eventually. But he'd already put up with more than his fair share of death, hadn't he? With just a minimum of luck he and Jody would have years and years together before they'd be facing that again.

Eventually he left off staring blindly into space contemplating his shocking good fortune. He went to the spare room where he changed from his dark suit to track pants and a T-shirt. Only then did he join his bride and Marybeth in the master bedroom.

"She's finished," Jody whispered from her recliner by the window.

Seth took the drowsy baby in his arms.

Jody held up the baby monitor, and he took it from her.

In the spare room, he put the monitor next to the blow-up bed. Then he burped and changed Marybeth. She was asleep by the time he positioned the pillows around her. He stood back for a moment to look at her, so sweet and peaceful, his now to love and protect.

In the master bedroom, Jody had already turned back the bed. As he stood staring at the snowy-white sheets, hardly daring to believe that in the morning he would wake up in that bed with her, he heard the bathroom door open behind him.

He turned. She stood in the doorway in a white, filmy bit of cobwebs and lace and nothing else. He could see the soft, womanly shape of her beneath the robe that wasn't really a robe at all. Her dark brown hair, warmed with red glints in the light from behind her, was loose on her shoulders. And her blue eyes were enormous, trained on his face.

"Jody." It came out like a prayer. Thankful. Sincere. And rough with yearning, too.

Her bare feet whispered across the rug and then she

was in front of him. He smelled her perfume, a little flowery, but also dark, like spice and sex. He wanted to grab her, yank her close, put his mouth and his hands all over her.

And yet there was a certain reverence within him, a reluctance to be as rough as his need for her demanded. "I'm afraid to touch you. Afraid I might..."

Her sweet mouth trembled on a smile. "Shatter into a million overexcited pieces? If so, I know the feeling."

"I was thinking more that I might hurt you. But yeah. What you said? That, too."

"Seth." She reached up a hesitant hand. Her finger brushed down the side of his throat, stirring sensations. Heat. Hunger. The promise of this night, of all their nights to come. "You won't hurt me." And then she went on tiptoe.

Her lips brushed his, back and forth.

Until he couldn't stand not to hold her good and tight in his arms. He grabbed her close.

She came up against him with an eager moan, and he claimed the kiss from her, deepening it, owning it. Her mouth opened beneath his, making way for his tongue to sweep in and taste the sweet and the salt of her. Her arms slipped up over his shoulders to encircle his neck. He felt her soft, full breasts pressed to his chest. He felt...

Everything, every curve, every inch of silky, cool skin, even the parts that were covered by that little bit of nothing she'd put on in the bathroom. He felt her all through him, in his blood, to the bone, her breath in his mouth and the warm satin of her hair against his cheek, the scent of her darker now, richer than ever. To him, she smelled like pure sex now. And he was rock hard and ready, aching to fill her.

"Yes," she whispered. "Seth…"

"Can't wait." He groaned the words against her parted lips.

"Yes," she said again, encouraging him when encouragement was the last thing he needed. "Oh, please. Everything…"

"Everything." He gave the word back to her as he took her down across the bed.

He should have been slow—he knew it. Slow and seductive and gentle and teasing.

But it had been so long and he ached so bad.

And she wasn't helping him to keep control.

"Now," she commanded, grabbing for his T-shirt, dragging it up and over his head. "Right now." She shoved at the track pants. He helped her, barely getting his erection free of the elastic waistband before she was pushing the pants over his hips and on down his thighs. He kicked to get out of them. They went over the side of the bed.

"Seth. Oh, my. All these muscles. And this…" She wrapped that cool, smooth hand around him. "Amazing."

"Jody. Jody, no!" He grabbed for her wrist.

She gave a low, needy moan that reached down inside him and stirred him all the hotter. "Let me…" And she tried to lower that smart mouth of hers onto him.

He couldn't let her do that. He would lose it completely if she did.

But then, well, it kind of looked like he would lose it anyway. He drove his fingers into the thick fall of her hair and grabbed on to keep her from taking him in.

"Ouch!" she cried.

"Sorry." He pulled her head up to him and kissed her lips, smoothing her hair as he did it, trying to soothe the pain that he'd caused. "Sorry, baby, but you were going to make me lose it…"

"So lose it." She made a low, growling sound. "I can't wait."

"Slow down…"

"No. Uh-uh. Later for that…"

He gave up trying to control it—control her. She was totally wild, and who was he to hold her back? He let her do what she wanted.

And what she wanted was frantic and beautiful, embarrassing and awkward and fine.

She grabbed that froth of cobwebs she was wearing and pulled at it until she got it above her waist.

He made the mistake of looking down then, getting an eyeful of all that womanly softness.

Bare. She was bare down there, completely revealed to him. The sight shocked him with a jolt of pleasure so strong, he almost erupted into climax right then and there.

"Jody!"

And she laughed, the sound naughty and bold and completely without shame, as she yanked the filmy nightgown over her head and tossed it away. "You like it?"

He pushed her gently to her back and rose up over her. And then he couldn't stop himself. He had to touch her, to feel the smoothness, to cup that bare mound and then to slide a questing finger along her slick, wet, unprotected folds. "Beautiful…" He groaned. He really was going to lose it, and she wasn't even touching him.

But she saved him from completely humiliating himself, saved him by wrapping one leg around him and then the other, by taking him in her hand again and guiding him into place.

He cradled her head on the pillow between his two hands. "Look at me while I come into you..."

The blue eyes, shining so bright, stared straight into his as he pushed in, as he tried with every ounce of will and restraint he had in him to take it slow for both their sakes. She'd had a baby not six weeks before, after all. He needed to be gentle with her. He needed to take care.

But she only smiled her naughty, knowing smile at him and wrapped her legs tighter around him. He sank into all that hot, wet softness.

It was sheer heaven, the best place a man could ever be.

"Kiss me, Seth."

Oh, and he did. He kissed her slow and deep and thoroughly, somehow managing to hold himself still for her, letting her find the pace and the rhythm that worked for her, though no way, at this point, would he be able to take her to the peak. This had to be way too fast for her.

But apparently, it was how she wanted it. She'd set this frantic, headlong pace—and not for herself.

For him.

She'd made this rough magic for him.

It didn't last long. He *couldn't* last long.

"Jody. I can't hold back..."

"Good." Her mouth slid away from his. She pressed her soft cheek to his beard-scruffy one. "Don't hold back." She breathed the command into his ear. "I don't want you to hold back..."

And that did it. His climax plowed through him, undeniable, unstoppable, painful in the best way, and mind-blowing, too.

His head filled with the scent of flowers and spice, he surged into her so hard and deep. And she took him, rode it out with him, murmuring heady encouragements, her soft hands stroking his back, her legs wrapped so tight around him, the whole of her claiming him, branding him as hers.

"Mrs. Yancy, that was not how I planned it," he confessed a few minutes later as they lay side by side. She had her hand on his chest, her head on his arm. He nuzzled her tangled hair and breathed in the sweet scent of her girlie shampoo.

"Mr. Yancy, that was perfect and don't you dare say otherwise."

He nipped her temple with his teeth. "Perfect for me, maybe."

She laughed, a low, sexy laugh that had him thinking he'd be ready to go again in no time. "There will be plenty of time for me. After all, we have a lifetime, right?"

"Yeah. Yeah, we do…" He touched her pink nipple.

"Careful," she warned.

"I don't mind."

"Sure?"

"Positive." He wanted to touch every inch of her. He cradled her breast in his hand and rubbed the nipple until a few drops of milk appeared.

"There's a towel." She kissed his shoulder. "In the nightstand drawer…"

He pulled the drawer wide and took out the hand

towel she'd stashed there. But then, after wiping up the moisture, he couldn't resist causing more, wiping that up, too, then dropping the towel in easy reach as he ran his fingers down the center of her, dipping one in at her navel, loving her softness, marveling at the silky texture of her skin.

And not only the look and feel of her, but the way she was as a woman, so open. Honest and lacking in pretense.

He'd liked that about her from the first, even when he'd been angry at her for not marrying Nicky, and for not seeking him out to tell him about the baby after Nicky died.

There were no coy games with Jody. She didn't open up easy, but when she did, she gave her all. She was strong and smart and serious. But with that edge, too, that sharp sense of humor, that toughness that came from the hard knocks she'd taken, the hard choices she'd had to make.

She fit him. Fit him in every way, including this. Fit him even better than Irene had...

Seth closed his eyes. Where had that disloyal thought come from?

"Seth?" Jody took his face between her hands. He opened his eyes reluctantly. She searched his eyes. "What is it?"

"Nothing," he whispered and kissed her.

"But..."

He kept on kissing her, nipping at her lips a little, spearing his tongue in, tasting all the slick, tempting places beyond her parted lips, until she went pliant and willing again.

"You went away there for a moment," she whispered.

"Right here," he replied and meant it. "Right here, with you, on our wedding night."

She smiled at him then, a glowing, open smile.

He returned to the pleasure at hand, tracing circles on her hip bones as she sighed and lifted toward his touch. *Mine*, he thought, as he went lower, down to where she was bare for him. He dipped his fingers in, loving the feel of her, wet and so willing.

She whispered his name, eased her legs wider. He deepened the caress, sliding two fingers in and then three, bracing up on an elbow so he could watch her face as she came apart for him that very first time, her mouth a soft O, her eyes glazed with pleasure.

"Seth." She wrapped her hand around his neck and pulled him down for a long, sweet kiss.

For a while, they drifted together, lazy and easy, whispering about nothing, sharing slow touches. Until she reached down between them again.

"Uh-uh." He took that naughty hand of hers and the other one, too, and raised them both above her head. "Keep these clever hands above your head. This time's for you."

"But I already—"

"Shh." He kissed her mouth, firm and quick. "I mean it. No hands."

Jody surrendered control.

Reaching, she found the top edge of the mattress and took hold. She let him do what he wanted with her.

And, oh, it was glorious, to be at his command. Those knowing fingers of his, warm and just rough enough, glided over her, stirring every last hungry nerve, making her body hum with need and yearning.

He bent close and he kissed her. Endless, arousing kisses that wiped her mind free of all rational thought. Kisses that began on her lips and then went lower.

And lower...

She looked down at him as he kissed her where she wanted him most. Her hands gripping the mattress for all she was worth, she lifted her body eagerly toward that wet, intimate caress.

He wasn't shy. He used his lips and his tongue and even his teeth to drive her higher. And those knowing fingers, too, he put them in play, until all she could do was moan his name and rock frantically, bucking her body to get closer to him.

And closer still...

And then at last, when he moved up her body again and she felt him, right there where she burned for him, pressing inside, she had no words fine enough for how good it felt.

It was exactly right, the way he came into her, slow and firm and steady, the gold in his eyes molten, his mouth swollen from kissing her, whispering her name rough and low. It was everything she'd given up hope of ever finding.

He was everything.

This man. A real man, her husband now. A man who shared his hardest secrets and listened when she told him hers. A loyal man who took care of her and her baby. A man who knew all the right ways to make her body burn.

She lifted her legs, wrapped them around him. It wasn't enough. "I need..."

Somehow, he knew. "Your arms, Jody. Put your arms around me now."

"Yes. Oh, Seth…" She let go of the mattress then and grabbed for him, twining her arms around him, too.

His big body pressed her down, and she pressed up to meet him. She held him so tight as he rocked into her, pushing her closer to the edge of sheer bliss.

Until, with a sharp cry, she went over, every nerve shimmering, a spiral of sparks and wonder lighting her up from inside as her climax burned through her.

And truly, she didn't mean to say it. She wasn't *going* to say it.

After all, he'd made it more than clear that everything he had was hers.

Everything but that.

But something broke with her climax, just broke wide open. And the truth she'd been denying came pouring out.

"I love you," she cried as her body pulsed around him. "Seth, I love you so much!"

Chapter Ten

He didn't say it back to her.

He didn't acknowledge the words, either.

Instead, he held her close. He kissed her endlessly. He treated her so tenderly, carrying her into the bathroom a little while later, filling the tub and sharing a lazy bath with her, then taking her back to bed.

Marybeth woke them at a few minutes after three in the morning. He went to get her. Jody nursed her there, in the bed, and then Seth carried her off to the spare room again, to change her and put her back down to sleep.

Jody lay alone, waiting for him, trying not to think too much about the three little words she'd said to him, about how he'd behaved as though she'd never said them at all.

What had she expected? For him to say them back to her?

No. She'd had zero hope that she'd get words of love from him. Because, even though they'd never actually discussed it, they were both clear on the love issue. She, Jody, had forever with him. They belonged to each other now.

But love?

Well, it wasn't exactly that love didn't enter into it.

It was only that he'd given his love already. He had to keep something just for Irene.

Jody reminded herself that she needed to be at peace with that. She'd known how it was with him when she said yes to him.

The next day, they went back to the ranch to spend some time with Bill, who was head-over-heels for his new granddaughter. They stayed for lunch and dinner, the men talking beef prices, alfalfa yields and fence repair. Jody puttered around the big, dated ranch house kitchen with Mae Califano. A grandmother several times over, Mae was as tall and lean as her husband, with thick gray hair and a ready smile.

Around seven that night, Jody, Seth and Marybeth returned to town.

Seth put Marybeth down in the spare room again and then came for Jody in the great room, scooping her up in his arms and carrying her straight to bed. He made love to her slowly the first time and hard and fast later. She reveled in every kiss, every lingering touch.

And she was careful not to let herself say her love out loud again. There was simply no point in going there. Again, she reminded herself that she'd said yes to him knowing that his heart was taken. She had no right to turn around and demand what he couldn't give.

She'd made her peace with the situation.

Or so she kept telling herself.

Monday at breakfast, Seth said he wanted to adopt Marybeth.

Jody wasn't surprised. "I think that's wise. My brother James is in family law. How about if I call him? I'll get us an appointment as soon as possible. We can get the process started."

Seth had just lifted a spoonful of oatmeal to his lips. He set it back in the bowl without eating it. "You're serious? Yes, you'll let me adopt her. Just like that?"

"What? You think I should argue with you about it?"

He knocked back a gulp of coffee. "I kind of thought I would have to convince you."

"Seth. If anything ever happened to me—"

"Don't even think it." He had visibly paled.

Her heart warmed. No, he wouldn't say he loved her. But she did matter to him. She mattered in the deepest way.

She made her tone softer. "I'm only saying that you're the one I would want for Marybeth, the one to stick by her, to look after her. You're already the dad that she needs. No matter what happens, you need a legal claim on her, too. I also think it's what Nick would want, to have the big brother he loved so much take care of his little girl."

Seth shoved his chair back hard enough that it went over with a crash.

"Seth!" Jody gasped as he rounded the table toward her. "Seth. What in the...?"

He grabbed her hand and pulled her up from her chair, sending it over backward, too. "Jody." He wrapped those big arms around her. "Jody…"

"What?" She stared up at him, bewildered.

"You amaze me, you really do."

She laughed then. "That's me. I aim to amaze."

His mouth swooped down and covered hers in a mind-bending, beautiful, never-ending kiss. He braced one arm at her back and bent to slide the other arm behind her knees.

"Seth!" she cried again, as he scooped her high against his chest and carried her to their bedroom, where he made fast, hot love to her, leaving her breathless and panting for more. They rested for a little while, and the second time was slower and infinitely sweet.

The next day, Tuesday, they visited Calder and Bravo, Attorneys at Law, to take the first step toward making Seth Marybeth's legal dad.

A week later, on Monday, Bill returned to Florida.

By then, Jody and Seth had already established a pattern for their daily lives. They stayed at the house in town during the week and went to the ranch on Saturdays and Sundays. The house in town was close to both Bloom and the justice center, so very little time had to be wasted driving back and forth to work. On the weekends, Seth could concentrate on whatever needed his attention at the ranch.

Jody loved the old ranch house. She wanted Marybeth to have a lot of good memories there, and she was already making plans to update the kitchen and redo the bathrooms—well, except for the big one upstairs with the claw-foot tub. That was perfect as it was.

The day after Bill left, Jody took Marybeth and met Elise for breakfast at the bakery.

"At last," said Elise. "You, me and morning coffee. Just like old times." From her stroller, Marybeth made a cooing sound. "I think you have the perfect baby."

"As of this moment, yes, I do. Let's savor the joy."

They talked about Elise's wedding, which was less than two weeks away now, with the ceremony to be held at Elk Street Community Church and the reception afterward at Justice Creek's famous and purportedly haunted Haltersham Hotel.

"So…" Elise swallowed a bite of blueberry muffin. "Married life? Good?"

"Crazy wonderful." *Except I said I love him and he didn't say it back.*

Not that she was letting herself dwell on that.

"I mean, you and Broomtail County's favorite lawman?" Elise widened her eyes and threw out both hands. "Whoever would have guessed? Except, when I see you together, it's so obvious. It's like you were meant for each other. Everyone says so."

"Everyone?"

"Clara, Nellie—me, of course." She added their sisters-in-law: "Addie, Chloe, Paige, Ava…"

"Seriously? You've all been discussing my relationship with Seth?"

"Of course. I mean, it happened pretty fast, but we all agree you're a great match. Seth is so self-contained, you know? And so are you. It's always been like pulling teeth to get you to admit when you're upset about something."

"Oh, come on. I'm not *that* bad."

"Yeah, you kind of are. But it's okay. We love you,

anyway. And I have to tell you, before you and Seth got together, he always seemed so unhappy, so depressingly grim. Polite and helpful, with a good head on his shoulders, the kind of guy you would want to have around to take things in hand during a natural disaster. But so stern. So serious. But then, last week at your wedding, I had a few minutes with him. He was charming and friendly. And, Jody, when he looks at you…" Elise fanned herself. "Whew. That guy is wild for you."

Not wild enough. The thought rose unbidden. Jody pressed her lips together to keep from saying too much.

But she must have given herself away. Elise leaned closer. "Jody, what's the matter?"

No. Bad idea to go there. What was Elise going to tell her that she didn't already know? Jody relaxed her shoulders, looked her sister straight in the eye and replied, "Not a thing. Why?"

"I don't know. For a moment there, I thought…"

"What?"

"There's really nothing bothering you?"

"Honestly. No."

Did she feel bad about lying to her sister? A little.

But really, how could it be lying when she *was* fine? She just needed to keep things in perspective, that was all.

But it ate at her, just chewed away at the edges of her happiness. She loved her husband, and she wanted him to love her back. And sometimes, when he kissed her or looked at her across the breakfast table in the morning, or asked her how her day had been when he got home from the justice center, she would know in her heart that he *did* love her. That, as fast as it had happened between them, from the night Marybeth was born until their marriage five and a half weeks later, she owned his heart as he owned hers.

That it was only the words he couldn't give her. Because he owed them to Irene and Irene alone.

Which, increasingly, pissed her the hell off.

She found herself understanding her mother better, of all things. Understanding what it was to love a man beyond all reason and know that he belonged to another. No, it wasn't the same, what her mother had done, fighting tooth and nail for all those years to steal another woman's husband.

It wasn't the same.

But still, Jody felt a certain kinship with her mother— or wait. Maybe it was Sondra Bravo Jody understood better now. She'd always wondered why Sondra never kicked Frank Bravo out on his sorry ass and filed for divorce.

Now she kind of got it. It was just possible that Sondra had loved Frank Bravo as passionately and possessively as Willow did. Sondra couldn't have her husband all to herself, but she clung to what she could have of him, anyway.

"What is going through that mind of yours?" Seth asked. He stood over her as she sat on the back steps at the house in town. It was nine at night and he'd just come out the sliding door after putting Marybeth to sleep in the spare room. They'd been married for two and a half weeks.

For a moment, Jody just sat there, facing away from him, staring off toward the back fence. Was this it, then, his invitation to talk about what she'd said on their wedding night?

She knew it wasn't.

"Why do you ask?" she said without turning.

"You've been kind of quiet all evening, that's all."

Jody turned and looked up at him, feeling that now-familiar ache of longing under her breastbone, wanting to get honest with him and at the same time just... not ready.

Not ready to go there, not ready to lay her heart on the line and then have to face the painful things he might say when she did.

She chose the coward's way. "I've been thinking we should go ahead and start putting Marybeth to sleep in her own room."

His bare feet brushed the porch boards as he came and sat beside her. He had the receiver for the baby monitor in his hand, and he set it on the next step down.

She waited for him to call her bluff, to insist that she get straight with him, tell him what was really on her mind.

He did no such thing. Instead, he wrapped his big arms around his spread knees and stared up at the night sky. "I thought you wanted her in the bassinet with us."

She studied his profile, his strong nose and hard jaw, the manly jut of his Adam's apple. A hint of his aftershave came to her, and a shiver of desire hollowed her out down low. "Seth. She's never in the bassinet with us. She's been sleeping in the spare room ever since we got married."

He slipped her a glance. The promise of the night to come thickened the air between them. Suddenly the little problem of loving him when he couldn't love her back seemed to matter a whole lot less than it had a minute before.

"We make a lot of noise," he said.

"Exactly. And I'm thinking we'll probably continue to do so."

"As long as I have anything to say about it, we will." He was looking straight at her now, a look that stole her breath and made her acutely aware of her blood as it pulsed through her veins.

"And that reminds me…"

"What?" He reached over and ran the backs of his fingers slowly down her bare arm. Nerve endings flashed and sizzled in response to that light touch.

What were they even talking about? *Focus.* "I want to fix up the room she's been sleeping in at the Bar-Y, too." The room was directly across the hall from the master bedroom, a nice, sunny space that faced the front yard. "I want to get her a crib there, paint the room in little-girl colors, set things up right for her there, too, so I don't always have to be hauling all her stuff back and forth."

"No problem." He slipped those caressing fingers under her hair and clasped the back of her neck. Better than a giant slice of Adriana Welch's chocolate cake, the feel of his hands on her flesh. "So, you're fine, then?" He pulled her in to him.

"Never better," she whispered as his mouth came down on hers.

And it was true, at that moment, as his fingers slid up into her hair, cupping the back of her head, holding her steady while he plundered her mouth.

It was true, as he slipped his other hand up under her tank top, clever fingers closing on her breast, kneading it until she moaned and felt her milk come in.

She pushed at his giant shoulders and looked down

at the dark spot on her shirt right over the curve of her breast. "Look what you did."

The hand in her hair slid lower. His fingers were warm on her nape, firm on her shoulder, arousing as they glided down her bare arm until he had hold of her hand. "Come inside with me. You can get out of that wet shirt."

She didn't argue. She might not have his love, but she owned that big body of his. When she held him in her arms, he belonged only to her.

He scooped up the baby monitor and rose, pulling her up with him, leading her back inside and straight to their bedroom. He set the monitor on the nightstand and got right to work getting her out of her clothes.

In about thirty seconds flat they were both naked, shirts and pants and underwear a tangled pile around their bare feet.

And then he grabbed her close again and put his mouth on hers, reaching down, those amazing hands curving under her bare bottom, lifting her.

With a moan of pleasure, she curled her arms around his neck and hitched up her legs to encircle his waist. His fingers moved, inching inward. And then he was touching her, opening her, readying her, his erection already hard and thick against her belly.

A cry escaped her. He drank it in—and then, out of nowhere, he broke the kiss.

She glared at him, wanting more. More kisses, more caresses, more of this wild beauty that pulsed between them. "What?" she demanded.

"You," he answered rough and low. "Everything."

Still standing, with her all wrapped around him, he slanted his head the other way and kissed her some more. She kissed him right back, heedless of their clothes trampled under his feet as his fingers worked their heady magic at her wet and eager core.

She was ready, beyond ready. Hooking her legs tighter around him, she lifted up and away to try to get him in place and take him inside.

He only chuckled and pulled her back to him, good and tight against his muscled heat, trapping his hardness between their bodies again. "Kiss me some more, Jody. Let's make it last…"

Jody held on. She kissed him forever as he went on touching her, driving her higher, making her burn.

Until she went over the edge of the world for him, letting her head fall back, whimpering at the ceiling, holding on to him for dear life as completion sang through every nerve.

Only then, so gently, did he lower her to their bed, only then did he come into her, gliding home to fill her. She sighed in pleasure as she took him in.

Once there, he stilled for a sweet, endless moment. And then he rolled them so she was on top, her legs folded on either side of him. "Ride me, Jody. Take me there."

She was only too happy to comply. Bracing her hands on his chest, she pushed her body up to a sitting position. It was so good this way—well, every way was good with him. But she loved looking down at him, watching the wonder and excitement on his face as she moved on him, rocking him slow and sweet. And then harder. Faster.

Until he lost it completely, grabbing her hips and pulling her down tight to him, spilling into her as he chanted her name.

Later, when he slept beside her, she reminded herself again of how good they were together, how she loved the life they shared.

And what were those three little words, really? Nothing but a certain arrangement of sounds.

No, he hadn't said them. But if she only stopped yearning for them, she could more fully appreciate all that he gave her, all that he was.

They shared so much. It should be enough.

She needed to remember that.

That following Saturday Elise married Jed. She had her three sisters, four sisters-in-law and her cousin Rory for her bridesmaids. Her lifelong friend, Tracy Winham, was her maid of honor.

The ceremony was at four with the reception at five thirty and expected to go well into the night. To start the day off right, Elise and her bridesmaids met at ten in the morning at Elise's favorite salon for hair and makeup.

Originally, Jody had planned to opt out of everything but the ceremony and maybe an hour or two at the reception afterward. She had Marybeth to consider. But Mae Califano volunteered to come in from the ranch and watch the baby at the house in town. That way, Jody could run home and nurse every four hours or so—or find somewhere private to pump if she had to.

It all went off beautifully, Jody thought. Elise wore a full-length white dress lavish with beads and lace and a cathedral-length veil. Flowers from Bloom filled the church. The bridesmaids wore teal blue satin, each in a different style. Annabelle Bravo, their brother Quinn's six-year-old, was the flower girl. Annabelle's best friend, Sylvie, carried the rings. Both Sylvie and

Annabelle wore fairy princess costumes complete with jeweled tiaras and filmy wings.

Elise and Jed had written their vows. An audible sigh went up from the guests when Jed confessed that he'd finally found happiness the day Elise knocked on his front door. He had more to say, all of it beautiful, full of love for his bride. He held Elise's hands and he looked in her eyes, and he promised to love her forever.

As Jed said his vows, Jody's sisters and sisters-in-law glanced out at the pews, looking for their husbands to share a quick glance of love and belonging. Jody did the same, her gaze seeking Seth.

His eyes were waiting. He gave her a slow smile. All that they had together—the passion, the mutual respect, the tenderness, the love for Marybeth—it all seemed to shimmer in the air between them.

It was a good moment. She turned back to the bride and groom reassured, somehow, that what she had with Seth was as real and as lasting as what Elise had with Jed, what Clara shared with Dalton, what Sylvie's mom, Ava, had with Jody's half brother Darius.

After the ceremony, there were pictures. When the photographer finally let them go, Seth drove Jody back to the house. They checked in with Mae. Jody nursed Marybeth, and then off they went again, this time to the hotel.

The weather was perfect, a little warm maybe, but not too bad. Snowy-clothed tables set with silver-rimmed china waited on the terrace, where dinner would be served. Cocktails, champagne and appetizers came first as everybody met and mingled. Then they settled in for the meal.

At seven thirty, the guests gathered in the ballroom

to watch the bride and groom share their first dance. After that, they could stay inside for more dancing or return to the terrace to visit without having to compete with the band.

The photographer called the wedding party together again—this time on the terrace as the sun began to set.

After that second round of pictures, Jody rejoined Seth in the ballroom. He tugged her close to his side and nuzzled a kiss against her hair. "Let's dance."

"You dance? Somehow, I never pictured you as the dancing type."

He gave her that slow smile of his. "I'm full of surprises."

"It's a fast one," she teased. "You sure?"

"I think I can manage to shuffle around."

Actually, that he was game for a dance delighted her. She followed him out onto the floor and they danced around each other like everyone else was doing.

After three fast dances, the band played a slow one. Seth pulled her close. She went happily into his arms, leaning her head on his shoulder as they swayed to that Ellie Goulding ballad from *Fifty Shades of Grey*.

What was it about him? In his arms she felt cherished and completely at home.

He rubbed his hand gently at the small of her back, sliding it up, stroking her hair, then caressing his way back down again, reminding her of what would happen between them that night when they were finally alone.

What she felt for him was like nothing she'd ever known before. She kept waiting for loving him to somehow become more ordinary, something accepted, like breathing. Something she could do without even having to think about it. It would be so much easier to love him that way.

He cradled her closer still. The woodsy scent of his aftershave seduced her. His lips brushed her temple.

Longing filled her.

All she wanted was everything. Was that so unreasonable?

She stifled a desperate laugh at the absurdity of her overwhelming desire, a laugh that could too easily have become a sob.

Truly, she only wanted what she'd given up hope of ever finding. Forever *and* his heart, too. Funny, that she'd had the words of love from Brent, but he never would give her forever.

With Seth, it was the other way around. Would she ever in her life manage both at the same time?

The truth she kept denying rose up within her. Really, this wasn't working.

It wasn't getting any better for her. She couldn't do it any longer, couldn't just wait around and hope that she would stop obsessing over loving him—or that he would somehow see the light, get past the awful events of seven years ago and openly return her love. She was going to have to figure out a way to make peace with herself, a way to somehow ease this awful feeling of being all bottled up inside.

She really did need to talk about it with him.

She needed to tell him she loved him—tell him calmly this time. Face-to-face. So he would have to acknowledge it, so he wouldn't be able to lie to himself that she'd only gotten carried away during a mind-blowing orgasm.

The song came to an end. They swayed to a stop.

She lifted her head from his shoulder and looked up into those warm amber eyes.

He gazed at her so tenderly. "My beautiful bride." And he tipped up her chin and brushed a kiss against her lips.

That did it.

The words rose up, demanding release. And she let them out for the second time. "I love you, Seth. I'm *in* love with you."

Chapter Eleven

His face went blank and his ears turned red.

Her heart shriveled to a dried-out raisin inside her chest.

And then, a moment later, he pulled it together. "Jody," he said, rough and low. Kind of chiding. As though she had wounded him by saying such a cruel thing. "Jody, you know that I care for you deeply, too."

I care for you deeply.

Ugh. Just…ugh.

Something clicked within her. A certain calm descended. "This isn't working for me. We have to talk about this."

He actually winced. "Now?"

The sense of calm deserted her as fast as it had come. Fury swept through her, heating her cheeks, making her heart race. It would have been much too satisfying to call him a bad name and run from the ballroom.

However, he did have a point. Elise's wedding was hardly the time or the place.

"You're right," she said. "We'll talk later." A fast song began. "For right now, keep dancing..."

It was after one in the morning when Jody thanked Mae and walked her out to her pickup.

Back inside, she could hear Marybeth starting to fuss.

Seth appeared from the great room holding the receiver for the baby monitor. "I'll get her."

"No. She'll want to nurse. I'll do it." She turned for the baby's room. Seth had moved her recliner in there.

She'd just settled in with Marybeth at her breast when he stuck his head in the door and asked, "Want me to change her?"

Jody shook her head. "I'll do it. Go on to bed."

He hovered there in the doorway, his tie undone, his eyes both wary and worried at once. All man. *Her* man—well, mostly. "Jody, I..."

"It's late," she whispered. "Get some sleep. We'll talk about it tomorrow."

He started to speak again, then seemed to think better of it. Tapping a palm on the door frame, he turned and disappeared down the hall.

A half an hour later, she settled her sleeping baby back in her crib, turned off the little lamp by her nursing recliner and tiptoed out into the hallway. The master bedroom door was open, but the light was off.

She actually dreaded going in there, but she made herself do it. Seth was already in bed, facing the far wall, the covers pulled up over his big shoulders.

Jody undressed in the bathroom. When she slid under the blankets with him, he didn't move.

Carefully, she settled on her side facing away from him, closed her eyes and waited for sleep to come and take her away from this too-quiet, dark room where the man she loved slept with his back to her.

In the morning, they ate breakfast in silence. She fed Marybeth and he changed her.

He had the whole day off, and so did she. They'd planned to head out to the ranch, but when he asked if she still wanted to go, she shook her head. "As soon as Marybeth goes to sleep, we'll talk. Then we'll see."

"What do you mean, we'll see?" He seemed angry, suddenly.

Well, too bad if he was upset. She wasn't all that happy with the current situation, either. "I mean, let's talk first before we decide what to do with the rest of the day."

"Jody—"

She showed him the hand. "*After* Marybeth goes to sleep."

Seth resented each minute as it ticked by. He didn't want to do this. They didn't need to talk—not about this. Not about love.

He'd thought Jody understood him, that she knew exactly where he came down on the question of love. But apparently, he'd gotten it all wrong.

By ten, Marybeth had conked out on her play mat in the great room. Seth carried her to her room.

When he came back out, he closed the door. Jody was the most reasonable woman he'd ever known. He didn't think things would get heated. But on the off chance that they did, well, no need to scare the baby.

Jody was waiting for him on one end of the sofa in the great room, looking way too good in skinny jeans that hugged every curve and a snug pink T-shirt, her bare feet up on the cushions, tucked to the side. He took the other end of the sofa.

For several awful seconds they both sat silent. Should he speak first?

He had no idea what to say. Whatever he came up with, he was just about certain she wouldn't like what he said.

Finally, she took the lead. "We never actually talked about love that night you asked me to marry you. We should have."

And he should keep his mouth shut now. He knew that. But he didn't. "Jody, I honestly thought you understood my position."

"I know. I thought I understood it, too. I thought I accepted it."

She did? "Then why are we doing this?"

She stiffened at his harsh tone. "You are not a stupid man, Seth Yancy. I know that you know what the problem is." She spoke each word way too clearly, like she was biting them off with her teeth. And then she paused for a very slow breath. "Love is important, Seth. Love matters. I love you."

I love you. It was the third time she'd said it. Every time she said it something happened inside him, a sense of triumph, a hot and wild spurt of pure joy—followed immediately by a hard slap of shame.

She said, "When I accepted your proposal, I knew I didn't have your love. I knew then as I do now that you feel you owe your love to Irene, because of what happened. Because she gave her life for yours. Is that wrong? Tell me if I've got it wrong."

He looked away. It hurt to hear her say it out loud like that. "If you understand, then why are we talking about it?"

"Because I *need* to talk about it. Because it's a hard thing, a really painful thing. And the hard and painful things are the ones we need to talk about the most."

He wasn't so sure about any of that—at least, not when it came to this particular hard, painful thing. And the more he thought about it, the more he hated the way she'd said the truth right out loud like that. Yes, he owed his love to Irene. But it sounded all messed up, somehow, when she put it in words. "It's just how it is, that's all."

She brushed his shoulder, so lightly, a touch that burned him to the core. "Look at me, please."

He made himself meet her eyes.

She scanned his face as if seeking points of entry. "I'm sorry, Seth. I misled you. I misled us both."

He didn't get it. The plain fact was that if anyone had done any misleading, it had been him. Because she was right. The night that he proposed, he'd never once said straight-out that his love was not included. Saying it out loud very likely would have been a deal-killer, and he'd known that at the time. He should be ashamed of that. And he was. Not ashamed enough to have done things differently, though.

He wanted her too much, needed her, really. With her, he had everything he'd never thought to have again. He would have done worse than just misleading her to get a yes out of her that night.

She said, "You're a wonderful man, and we fit together, you and me."

"Exactly."

"We're suited to each other. The way we are together, the way our lives mesh, I never thought I was going to find that with a man. I mean, with you, doing everyday things is…fulfilling. Exciting. Just all-around *right*. So I wanted you, wanted to be with you. I couldn't wait to be your wife."

Cautiously, he suggested, "All that sounds really good."

She nodded. "It *is* good."

"And it's the same for me. I don't see the big problem."

"The problem is that I said yes too soon."

"No. Not true."

"Yeah. I wanted everything you offered me, the two of us together, building a good life, raising Marybeth. And maybe other babies if it worked out that way. I still want it all, Seth. Everything you offered me. That isn't going to change." She reached out—and hesitated just before she touched him. Her hand fell to her thigh.

"Jody—"

"Wait. Please. The truth is, I want what we have, and I'm happy. But I want your love, too. I can accept that Irene will always have a claim on your heart. I respect that. I think that's beautiful and right. But you have to make room for me in there, too. That's what marriage is. We stood up together in front of Pastor Jacobs and promised to love and honor each other. *Love*, Seth. It was right there in our wedding vows."

He didn't know what to say to her. "Jody. I told you. I do care for you."

Her lip curled, and not in a smile. "Okay, now you're starting to tick me off."

"What? I don't—"

"Don't give me that *I care for you* crap, Seth. I know that you *care* for me. You *care* for me in a thousand ways, and I love every one of them. But your *care* for me is not what we're talking about here."

"I just…" He stood. "I can't talk about this anymore. There's just no point."

She tipped that beautiful face up to him, her soft mouth set. "You may be right."

He didn't like the sound of that. "What are you saying?"

A frown creased the smooth space between her eyebrows. "I don't know. I'm not sure."

"Jody, dear God in heaven. What we have is good."

She rose, too, unfolding those fine legs to stand and face him. "I know it is, Seth." Her voice was soft now, almost tender. "I love you. I do."

There it was again—a flash of heat, a stab of shame. "We'll be all right."

"I don't know."

"You don't know? Why are you talking like this? You're my wife. Of course you know. We'll work it out. That's what married people do." Or what they *should* do, anyway.

Now he was thinking of his mother, all those years ago, running off with some drifter and never coming back. Not a lot of working-things-out going on there.

Jody said, "I would like you to give what I've said some serious thought. It might not hurt to find someone to talk about it with."

He glared down at her. "Someone to talk with?"

"That's right. I think talking to someone else about this could be a good thing for you."

How was this happening? The whole world was spinning right out of his control. "A psychiatrist, is that what you mean? I don't need a shrink."

"If you're uncomfortable with a professional, maybe call your dad or talk to Roman or Pastor Jacobs…"

His dad. She wanted him to call his dad about this? Not happening. And Roman? Even worse.

As for Pastor Jacobs…

No.

Just no.

"I'll think about it," he said. And he would. Way too much. Not that thinking about it would have him running to Pastor Jacobs to spill his guts. When a man had problems, he worked them out himself.

And for now, well, he didn't need to stand here and listen to her hint that she might be planning to leave him. "Is that all, then?"

"Think about what I've said. Please?"

He couldn't take anymore. He had to get out of there. "I'm going out to the Bar-Y. You coming?"

"No. You go ahead." She speared her fingers in her silky hair and raked it back from her forehead. "I could use a little time to myself, anyway."

Jody cleaned the house that day. She did laundry. She roasted a chicken with new potatoes for dinner, though she had her doubts that Seth would return for the meal.

But he did return.

And when he came back, he was calm and so kind. He praised the meal and talked about the new tractor he and Roman were thinking of buying. He took over with the baby the way he always did, changing diapers, walking her, whispering to her, cuddling her while he watched the Rockies game.

In bed, he pulled Jody close. She went to him with a yearning sigh. She gloried in his kiss, in his every caress. Their lovemaking was urgent and better than ever.

Afterward, he held her close. She tipped her head back and kissed him. "I love you," she said and prayed that a miracle might happen, and he would say it back to her.

Or at least, that he might be willing to talk about the problem some more.

Her prayers were not answered.

He said, "Good night, Jody." And he reached over and turned off the light.

Monday was more of the same. He was attentive and warm to her at breakfast. When he got home that night, he was helpful and kind.

They reached for each other when they went to bed. He entered her slowly. The heat between them burned high. It was heaven, just to be held in his arms.

But when she told him she loved him, he did not say it back—or even acknowledge that she'd said it at all.

Same thing on Tuesday. A whole lot of mutual civility between them, but every word felt empty. He was in the same room, but a million miles away from her.

That night, she went to bed early. When she got up to feed Marybeth, he was sleeping beside her, a big lump under the covers, facing the wall.

Wednesday, it got worse. They didn't talk. He ate breakfast, carried his dishes to the sink and left her there to finish up her bacon and eggs alone.

The distance between them was growing. She had to do something.

That night, at dinner, she said, "I've been thinking about what we discussed on Sunday…"

He put up a hand. "Don't go there, Jody. There's just no point."

Tears scalded her throat and burned behind her eyes. But she'd be damned if she let them fall.

Uh-uh.

She finished her dinner in silence, put the dishes in the dishwasher and went to bed early again.

Thursday, she met Elise at the bakery for breakfast. They talked about the honeymoon Elise and Jed were planning. As soon as Jed finished the novel he was working on, they would fly to Paris for three weeks.

Elise sensed that things weren't right with Jody.

"You know you're going to need to talk about it eventually," Elise said as she cut her muffin into quarters and then blotted up the crumbs with her fork. "Whatever it is, I'm here and I'm listening."

Jody cut a bite of her cinnamon coffee cake and then didn't even feel like eating it. She felt so low, she had trouble pretending that nothing was wrong. "I can't talk about it now, but you're the best and I love you."

"When you're ready, let me know. I'm here."

"I know. And I will." She hoped it wouldn't come to that. But things weren't getting any better between her and Seth. At some point, she was going to need to talk it out with someone. Elise would most likely be the one.

Or maybe Nellie. Or Clara. Or Ava or Rory.

Actually, it cheered her up just to think of her sisters, of all the women of her family by blood and by marriage. When she needed them, they would be right there.

As fed up as she was with Seth, she ached for him that he seemed to have no one he would tell his secrets to.

He used to tell them to her.

But since she wouldn't stop repeating her unbearable words of love to him, he was telling her nothing.

Nothing at all.

And she, well, she totally resented this crap he was giving her.

He had it all wrong. And he had to know that. What man did that? Told a woman she could have everything from him, all that he was and all that he owned.

Just not his love.

That hurt. It was a blow straight to her heart. And every time she said she loved him and got nothing back, he just drove the pain deeper.

The pain made her angry.

And she was mad at herself as much as at him. She *had* known where he stood on the question of loving that night he asked her to marry him. She'd known, but she'd said yes, anyway. She really was a complete fool when it came to love.

It had to stop. They needed, somehow, to work it out.

But again that night, they slept turned away from each other, each clinging to their separate sides of the bed.

Friday night it was the same.

Saturday, she took Marybeth and went to Bloom for a few hours. When she got back to the house, he was still at the justice center. He showed up at a little after one and went straight to the spare room to put away his service weapon and badge in the safe he'd installed there.

A few minutes later, he appeared in the great room, where Jody was folding laundry, with Marybeth in her bouncy seat on the floor. He picked up the baby and patted her back. She cooed in contentment that Daddy was home.

"I'm going out to the Bar-Y," he said. "Will you come with me?" He looked so tired. She ached for him.

And for herself. "Sure." She planned to go into Bloom the next day for a couple of hours. "I'll need my own car, so I'll follow you in the Tahoe."

At the ranch, he went off with Roman to look for a missing calf. She hung out with Mae. They all had dinner together, and then Mae and Roman went back to their house across the yard.

By eight, Marybeth was asleep in her freshly painted and furnished room. Seth sat in the family room staring at the TV.

And Jody?

She just couldn't take it anymore. Not one more night marooned on her side of the bed. Uh-uh. Not doing that.

In the big master bedroom that looked out on the backyard, she got out the suitcase she'd stored in the closet a couple of weeks before and filled it with random items of clothing she'd been leaving at the ranch since she and Seth got married. There were a few things in the baby's room she needed, too, but she would grab those just before she went out the door.

She rolled the suitcase into the family room. Seth glanced over and saw her.

The suitcase got his attention. He pointed the remote. The TV went dark. "Jody," he said wearily. "What are you doing?"

"This isn't working." She launched into the little speech she'd been rehearsing as she packed. "I think we need a break. I'm going back to the other house, and I want you to stay here. For a while. Until we find a way to work things out."

He stood and demanded, "You're leaving me?" He took a step in her direction.

She put up a hand and he stopped. "No, Seth. I'm not leaving you. I told you, I'm taking a break."

His eyes burned right through her. "Leaving won't solve anything."

"Maybe not. But I'm not spending another night with you like this. I'm going to put this suitcase in the Tahoe and then get Marybeth—and don't worry. I know you'll want to see her. So I'm thinking you can stop by a few hours a day at the other house. Call me tomorrow. We can work that out."

He moved a step closer. "This isn't right."

"If you take another step I'm going to say stuff you won't like."

He froze. "Jody. Don't go." And then he did what she'd warned him not to. He took another step and another. Until he was standing right in front of her, smelling of soap from the shower he'd taken before dinner—soap and that woodsy aftershave of his. And man.

All man.

Her man that she desperately needed a break from.

She swallowed hard and glared up at him. "I warned you."

And then he made it worse. He lifted his big hand and cradled the side of her face. His touch burned as hot as his gaze on her. "Jody…"

She knocked his hand away and jumped back. "You need to do some thinking, Seth. You need to decide if you're going to be mine or not. I know you loved her. And I know your guilt runs bone-deep, that she died and you weren't able to save her. But this thing you have, this *rule* you have about not having any love for me, about saving all your love for her? It's a rotten rule, Seth. And I'm not going to live my life with some bad rule of yours sucking all the joy from every moment we have together."

"Jody, stay."

"No."

"Jody, please." His voice was so gentle now. Full of love—or whatever it was he felt for her that couldn't be love because he loved a dead woman and not her.

"Uh-uh. Not like this." Bracing herself against the temptation to soften toward him, she rolled the suitcase around in front of her, making it a barrier between them.

"Walking out on me solves nothing."

"Maybe not. But I need to go."

"Jody, you said it yourself. You knew the situation when you married me. I want you. I *like* you. I'm happy with you—or I was, until just lately. We can have everything together. Why can't you see that?"

"What I see is it's *not* everything if your love gets saved for her."

"Jody, be reasonable."

"Reasonable? Forget that. I'm not feeling reasonable, and I'm also not through. It's…it's ridiculous, is what it is. You've, what? Had your great love and you can't love again? Please. It's what I said. It's crap, as big a bunch of crap as your other rule about not dating women from town. And you know what? I might have put up with it. I might have let it go, gotten over it, given you time to come to trust and believe in what we have together, given you time to finally let her go—but no. You had to make it crystal clear that you're *never* getting over her. You had to be sure I understood that twenty years from now, I'll be loving you with everything I have in me to love—and you'll still be cutting me out, telling me you *like* me and *want* me and I'm *yours*, but as for loving me? So sorry, Jody. Out of luck there."

His ears were bright red, and his face had gone ghost pale. "That's not fair."

"Fair?" She leaned over the suitcase to wave her hand in his face. "Oh, come on. You don't even want to start lecturing me about what's fair. I waited my whole life for you, and if you think I'm settling for less than all of you, you need to think again." She grabbed the handle of the suitcase and turned for the door.

He didn't try to stop her.

Which was just as well. She'd said all she had to say to him. For now, she just needed to throw the suitcase in the Tahoe, grab the baby and return to the empty house in town where she could nurse her broken heart in peace.

Chapter Twelve

For the past few days, Seth had believed that it couldn't get any worse between him and Jody.

But now she'd taken Marybeth and returned to town without him.

Yeah. Okay, he got the picture now.

It not only *could* get worse. It just had.

And she'd left in a fury. Had she been careful driving home? He shut his eyes to block out the sudden graphic image of her Tahoe wrapped around a tree.

He made himself wait a half an hour before he called to be sure she'd gotten back to the house safely.

"I'm fine," she said, her voice flat, disengaged. "Thanks."

"I...left my badge and the Glock in the safe there."

"Come and get it tomorrow. And anything else here you need."

You. I need you and I need Marybeth. "Can I see Marybeth, too?"

"Of course. Three o'clock?"

"I'll be there."

"See you then." And before he could think of what to say to keep her on the line, she was gone.

He stared at the TV for a while and then went upstairs to face his bed without her in it.

The next day crawled by. It seemed like three o'clock would never come.

He knocked on the door of the house where he used to live like some stranger come to visit. She answered with Marybeth in her arms. He stood there and stared at her, at her blue eyes that saw too much, at her mouth that he wondered if he'd ever get to kiss again.

She stepped back to let him in and then handed him the baby. Marybeth made a small, happy little sound.

"How've you been, sweetheart?" He kissed her fat little cheek, and she cooed as he laid her against his shoulder. The pain and lack that had dogged him all day eased a little.

"I have a few errands to run," Jody said. "I'll be back in two hours."

Wait. She was leaving? "You don't have to go."

Her mouth tightened. But all she said was "I just fed her. See you." And she grabbed her purse and phone from the table by the door and left.

When she got back she wanted to set a regular time for him to visit.

How about every night, all night, and mornings and weekends? How about you just let me come home?

But of course, that wouldn't fly, so he asked for evenings. He could come over from the justice center once he was done for the day before heading back to the ranch for the night.

"Eat before you show up," she said. "Please."

That cut him deep. "You don't even want to eat with me?"

She took a slow breath before she answered. "The whole point is to have a break. People taking a break don't eat together."

He couldn't resist a show of sarcasm. "I didn't know there were rules for this."

"Well, there are. Just like *your* rules about loving— or *not* loving, as the case may be."

About then, Marybeth must have picked up the tension between them. She started to fuss.

Jody said, "Let's not stress out the baby. See you tomorrow night."

She opened the door for him and ushered him out.

The next night he brought dinner with him anyway, in spite of her *rule*. He offered to share. She just picked up her phone and purse and said she'd be back in a couple of hours.

It went the same on Tuesday night. She left as soon as he arrived and shooed him out the door the minute she got back.

By Wednesday, he was starting to wonder why he didn't just go ahead and say it to her. Would that be enough for her, if he just said, *I love you*?

Unfortunately, he knew he couldn't do it—or at least, that if he did manage to choke the words out, he would only sound like a bald-faced, despicable liar. And that would only make her all the more determined to keep on as they were.

As they were? It was awful. He couldn't believe he'd lived like this for all those endless years. He wanted his wife back, wanted his *life* back, the life he'd created with her, the life with laughter and honest talk between them, with great sex and her soft, curvy body in his arms while they slept.

By Friday afternoon, it was so bad he was starting to admit that maybe Jody was right.

He had a problem, one he hadn't made himself solve for seven years. The problem had worked for him. It was an excellent and effective way to punish himself for what had happened to Irene.

But then along came Jody. And now, when he punished himself, he was hurting her, too.

He needed to talk to her about it.

But when he picked up the phone, he set it right back down. Because just admitting he had a problem wasn't enough.

What was she supposed to do with that information?

It still remained *his* problem to solve.

She'd said he should talk to Pastor Jacobs or a therapist or maybe his dad. What were they going to tell him that he didn't already know?

As he picked up the phone again, he realized it was time to find out.

Jody wanted Seth back.

Every time he showed up at the door, it got harder not to throw herself into his arms.

Still, she held out, held back. She reminded herself of

the hardest truth: it wasn't going to work if she couldn't have his heart.

Friday night, he seemed different, somehow. Quieter, more at ease. He didn't bring dinner to share, didn't try to get her talking the way he'd done every other night that week, didn't offer to take the Tahoe in for service the way he had two days before.

He took Marybeth from her arms and asked, "So, where are you off to tonight?"

"Dinner with my sisters and Rory at the Sylvan Inn." She'd set up the meeting and would pick up the check. "I'm going to tell them about my little boy."

He studied her for a moment, his expression hard to read—accepting maybe? Even pleased? "Why now?"

"I don't know. It seems like it's about time, that's all."

He gave her a slow nod, but didn't say anything else.

She caught herself about to lean up for a kiss. "Well. See you in a while."

"Take your time. I'll be here."

An hour and a half later, Jody sniffed back tears as the waitress—not Monique Hightower, thank God— set three gorgeous desserts and a handful of spoons on the table. She then poured them coffee, served Jody tea and left them alone.

Nellie dug right into the tiramisu. "I can't believe that *Ma* knew."

Jody sniffled. "Yeah, it's scary when you think about it. She's a lot more perceptive than she lets on."

Clara handed Jody another tissue. "You all right, Jo-Jo?"

"I'm still sad about it. I always will be." Jody blew her nose. "But I really do feel I did the right thing."

Across the table, Elise dabbed at her eyes, too. "I get why you didn't tell us then. Some of us were downright evil at the time." She pointed her thumb at herself and pulled a long face.

"You weren't *that* bad," said Nellie. Elise shot her a look, and Nellie relented. "Okay, you were pretty bad."

They all laughed through their tears.

And then Rory said, "I know you're going to work it out with Seth."

Nell tasted the lava cake. "I still don't get what the problem is." Jody had only said that they were having issues, taking some time apart. "What *issues*, exactly?"

Clara reached over and ran a hand down Nell's fabulous auburn hair. "I don't think we're getting details, honey."

Nellie wrinkled her perfect nose at Clara. "Hey, a girl can hope."

"And we're here for you, remember that," said Elise. "Anytime. Whatever you need."

A chorus of agreement went up from the others.

Jody wiped her eyes again. "I hit the jackpot when it comes to sisters, that's for sure. Cousins, too." She gave Rory a wobbly smile and raised her teacup high. "And here's to our sisters-in-law." They all lifted their cups. "To Addie and Ava, Chloe and Paige."

Nellie tried the crème brûlée. "Omigod. This is the best. Pick up your spoons, my sisters. You need to taste this, and I need *not* to eat it all myself."

"How'd it go?" Seth asked, turning off the TV and rising from the sofa.

"It was good. Really good. It feels right that I told them."

"I'm glad." He picked up his phone from the table at the end of the sofa. "Tomorrow I've got some things I have to deal with."

Things he had to deal with? What did that even mean?

Not that it was any of her business. They were taking a break from their marriage. That meant neither of them had to explain their activities to the other.

A break from their marriage?

Who'd come up with that brilliant idea?

Oh, right. *She* had.

He added, "So I think I'll have to skip the visit tomorrow. Unless you need me to—"

"No. No, really. That's fine. Sunday at three, then, same as last week?" Had they only been doing this for a week? It seemed like a lifetime to her.

"Three's good." He turned for the door.

She followed him to her small square of entry hall. "Good night, then."

"Night, Jody." He went out the door.

She shut it behind him and leaned back against it with a heavy sigh.

Seth was waiting on the front steps of the ranch house at 2:15 p.m. the next day when the rental car rolled into the yard. He got up and went down the steps.

The blue sedan pulled to a stop, and the trunk popped open. Seth grabbed the small suitcase from inside as Bill Yancy got out and shut the door. Roman's dog, Toby, came bounding over.

Seth's dad bent to greet him. "Hey, Toby. How's my good boy?"

The dog panted and wiggled in delight as Bill scratched him around the ruff of the neck.

Seth said, "Long flight just for a conversation."

His dad rose to his height. "I'm retired. I can go where I want when I want. And some conversations oughtta be had face-to-face." He reached out his arms. Seth put down the suitcase and went into them. They slapped each other on the back and stepped quickly apart.

From the porch of the foreman's cottage, Mae called, "Hey, Bill!" Seth's dad waved, and Mae whistled for Toby, who barked once and ran back the way he'd come.

Seth picked up the suitcase and led the way inside.

Two hours later, Bill was all settled in one of the rooms upstairs. He'd had a little nap and a sandwich. It was a sunny day. Seth got a couple of cold ones from the fridge, and they went out to the back porch, where they sat in the pair of black walnut rocking chairs that Seth's great-grandfather had made back before he died in the Battle of Belleau Wood during World War I.

"Where even to start?" Seth took a long pull off his beer.

His dad didn't say anything. Bill Yancy had always known how to wait.

Finally, Seth started talking. He talked about Irene, about her death, about the promise he'd made himself that there wouldn't be anyone else for him. "But then along came Marybeth. And Jody. And everything changed." He spoke of his happiness. And the words of love he felt he couldn't give his wife. "And now she's gone. We're taking a break, she says. She's not going to take me back until I can say I love her and mean it."

"Well, *do* you love her?"

Seth opened his mouth, then closed it and shook his head. "I don't mean no. I just mean…" Seth swore. It was one of those words he never let himself say, but the moment seemed to demand that word, somehow. "I don't even know what I mean."

Bill sipped his beer. The old rocker creaked as he leaned back. "I'm going to tell you something now."

Seth slanted his dad a look. "Something helpful?"

"Well, that's my hope. And while I'm telling you, I want you to think how I always said that above all, a Yancy is loyal."

"You've always been that, Dad, loyal to the core."

"Yeah." Bill didn't sound especially pleased with the fact. "I fell in love with Darlene when you were seven years old."

Seth took a moment to let that sink in. "But you never brought her home until I was fourteen. I was fifteen when you married her."

"That's right. By the time I brought her and Nicky to meet you, I had been in love with her for seven years. I met her first when she worked at Ames Bank, before she got that waitress job at the diner. I used to go in that bank and make extra deposits and withdrawals just to see that smile of hers."

Seth had started to catch on. "But you were still thinking my mother would come back."

"That's right." Bill rocked and the old chair creaked. "Carlotta had run off when you were barely walking. I should have divorced her by the time I met Darlene. But no. I had my ingrained Yancy loyalty to live by. I was a married man, and it was my duty to wait for my wife to come home. Then came the day that Darlene asked me out. I passed her two twenties and a deposit slip across the counter between us and she gave me that beautiful smile of hers and said, 'Bill Yancy, let's go to the movies, just you and me. What do you say?'"

Seth swallowed hard against the lump in his throat. "I miss Darlene."

"Son, you are not alone—and where was I? Ah, yes. Darlene asked me out and that scared me to death, I wanted it so bad. But by then, I'd been telling myself for six years that Carlotta would come home. I'd never gotten a divorce. I *was* a married man. I told Darlene I couldn't. And then I turned around and left that bank and never went back. I started banking at Wells Fargo, and I set my mind on not thinking of Darlene Sampson's beautiful smile ever again. Four years after I ran from the bank where she worked, I heard she started going out with Kirk Couch. I knew that guy was trouble and I didn't like it, but I was a married man and had no right to say anything about what Darlene Sampson did. And then she went and married Kirk. And then he left her, ran off just like Carlotta had done to you and me, left her with a sweet little boy and nothing much else. I got my divorce then, and Darlene got hers. The rest you pretty much know."

Seth didn't much like the comparison his dad seemed to be making. "My mother walked away from us and never looked back. Irene died saving me. No way is that the same."

"Course it's not. Your Irene and Carlotta were nothing alike. But you and me? You not only got that Yancy look from me, you got that sense of loyalty so strong it can lead you astray if you're not careful."

"Loyalty is a good thing, Dad."

"I can't argue that point. What I *can* say is that I

threw away seven years of happiness because I wouldn't stop clinging to something that was long gone. I think about that, son. I think about it a lot. Seven years I lost in misery, seven years I could have been spending with my beautiful Darlene. Yeah, I think about Nicky, too. That without my pigheaded foolishness and those seven years wasted, we wouldn't have had Nicky, and I can't imagine a world that never had Nicky in it. But still. Darlene's gone now. And the hard fact is that I could have had seven more years with her if I'd only had my head on straight. What will you be thinking when Jody is gone?"

"Damn you, Dad. Don't say stuff like that."

Bill stopped rocking. "Tell me, Seth Patrick Yancy, is Irene Vargas ever coming back?"

"Of course not."

"Do you think she died so that you could be unhappy?"

"What are you saying?"

"Irene died so you could live, boy. Think about that. Think about what she gave for you. Think about Jody and Marybeth, who are living and breathing and in need of your love and tender care. Ask yourself if the way you're behaving honors a fine woman's sacrifice."

Bill left the next day.

Seth walked him out, put the suitcase back in the trunk of the blue sedan and closed the trunk lid. He went around to the open driver's-side window. "I wish you'd stay."

"Not this time."

"Think about coming back home to live, Dad."

"I like Florida. The blue, blue sky. The palm trees

and white sand beaches with the waves sliding in. And it's been easier, not to be where everything reminds me of Darlene."

"You might change your mind, though. We miss you here."

"I gotta admit, I've always been a family man. You work things out with Jody, I might be tempted to come on home and practice bein' a grandpa full-time."

"I love you, Dad. Thanks."

Bill gave a quick nod. "Proud of you, son. Never forget that." And then he started up the car.

Seth stood back to watch his father drive away.

Five minutes later, the blue sedan was long gone, and Seth was still standing there in the yard beside the cruiser he'd driven home the day before. He was thinking about Jody, about all the things he needed to say to her. He was hoping he could somehow make her see that he was finally ready to be the man she needed him to be.

It was one of those Sundays.

Lois was on the schedule for that day, but she had some weird virus and called in sick. Jody called Marlie and got lucky there. Marlie went in to open up.

But then Bloom's Sunday delivery driver, Bobby Krebstall, didn't show up. When Marlie tried to call him, he didn't pick up and didn't call back.

So at ten thirty, Marlie called Jody, who packed up a fussy Marybeth and drove to the shop, where she discovered that Bobby, who'd worked the day before, had driven the delivery van home. So, not only no driver, but no van to deliver the orders in.

Bobby was so done working for Bloom. Jody tried

the two drivers they used during the week, but neither could come in that day.

It could have been worse, she reminded herself as she sat in the office in back nursing Marybeth and hoping the baby would stop fussing so much. There weren't that many deliveries, and she could make them in the Tahoe.

At two thirty that afternoon, Marybeth was crying in her car seat, and Jody had one more delivery to go. Sweet old Mr. Watsgraff and his wife were celebrating their fiftieth anniversary. They lived in a small, new development not all that far from the turnoff to the Bar-Y. Mr. Watsgraff wanted the usual white roses, but this time he'd ordered three dozen and sprung for a gorgeous Tom Stoenner art glass vase.

All day, as she'd alternately soothed her unhappy baby, helped Marlie in the shop and headed out to make deliveries, Jody had kept thinking she ought to call Seth and warn him that she might be late to meet him at the house. Actually, he would have come to her rescue in a New York minute and appeared at the shop to do Marybeth duty for as long as she needed him if she'd only asked him.

But she didn't like asking him for things. She didn't like how damn wonderful he was with her, with her baby—okay, fine. *Their* baby. After all, he would be Marybeth's legal father as soon as the adoption went through.

But whatever she called him vis-à-vis Marybeth, she *didn't* want to call him on the phone and admit that she needed him. She wanted *him*, all of him, damn it, including his stubborn heart and those all-important three little words spoken out loud and clear and without hesitation.

However, she didn't have what she wanted, and she was starting to fear that she never would. She'd made her big stand, and they were living separately. And as far as she could make out, he still felt he owed his love to a dead woman.

Marybeth yowled.

"It's okay, sweetheart." She sent a quick glance over her shoulder at the sobbing baby. The car seat was pointed backward, but Jody could clearly see her baby's red cheek and angry, open mouth and her little fist waving. "It won't be long now. Mommy just has this one more delivery, and then I'll take you home to Daddy."

Marybeth only wailed louder.

Jody gritted her teeth and turned onto the street where the Watsgraffs lived.

She parked in the Watsgraffs' driveway, leaving the windows down a crack so the baby would have fresh air for the three minutes it took to carry the flowers inside. At 2:35, she set the vase full of roses on the Watsgraffs' dining room table. Mrs. Watsgraff was teary-eyed. Mr. Watsgraff beamed.

Jody wished them the happiest anniversary ever and got the hell out of there.

In the Tahoe, Marybeth was still crying. Jody opened the door behind the passenger seat and leaned in to check her diaper. Dry. As a rule, Jody tried not to depend on pacifiers. But some days, well, what was a harried mom to do?

She got one out of the pocket of Marybeth's diaper bag and slipped it into the baby's crying mouth.

Marybeth blinked in what truly did look like outrage. And then she opened her mouth wide. The pacifier dropped out. Jody tried to poke it back in again, but her baby was having none of that.

In the end, Jody gave up and stuck the pacifier back in the diaper bag. "Just a few minutes longer, sweetheart," she coaxed. "You'll be with Daddy. You'll feel better then."

Marybeth cried all the louder. Again, Jody considered calling Seth to let him know she could be late. But then, if she got on the road immediately, she could make it in time.

Jody shut the door and went around to the driver's side. She climbed behind the wheel and got going, observing the speed limit until she left the Watsgraffs' development, but pressing the gas a little harder than she should have once she got out on the open road.

She was maybe ten minutes from town and making great time when a lovely thing happened. Marybeth stopped crying. Jody glanced at her in the rearview mirror. She was sound asleep, her little head turned to the side, looking exhausted and adorable, a shiny bubble of drool on her pouty rosebud mouth.

Jody started to smile—but then through the back windshield she saw the flashing lights.

"Crap." She'd only been going a few miles over the speed limit. Some days a girl just couldn't catch a break.

The cop behind her turned on his siren, too.

"You have got to be kidding me..."

The siren wailed louder.

"Fine," she muttered. "All right. I'm pulling over." She slowed, steered to the shoulder and stopped.

Behind her, the siren wound down to nothing, but the lights kept on flashing. Tires crunched gravel as the cruiser slid in behind her.

She didn't realize it was Seth until he emerged in his khaki uniform, aviator sunglasses and Smokey the Bear hat. He shut the cruiser's door, adjusted his sunglasses and came right for her.

She rolled down her window but stayed in the car. Wasn't that what you were supposed to do when an officer of the law pulled you over—even if the officer in question just happened to be the guy you were married to?

He leaned in the window, bringing that infuriatingly wonderful scent of soap and man. "Going a little fast there, young lady."

She took off her own dark glasses and tossed them on the passenger seat before hitting him with a look cold enough to freeze the testicles off a polar bear. "Is this supposed to be funny?"

"Not wise to use that smart mouth on an officer."

God. That sounded downright dirty. What did he think he was doing, anyway?

She turned her gaze straight ahead and told herself things could be worse. At least Marybeth hadn't started screaming again. Yet. "It's been a hellacious day, Seth. I was hurrying to get to the house in time to meet *you*, in case you've forgotten. And I'm not in the mood for—"

"Ma'am. I want you to step out of the car."

Wow. Had he lost his mind? It seemed increasingly possible.

"You do remember that you were coming to see Marybeth at three?"

"I remember. Step out of the car, miss."

"What is the matter with you?" She pushed the words out through clenched teeth.

He moved back from the door a step and crossed his arms over his chest. "I'm not going to ask you again."

Ha. As if there had been any *asking* going on. "Fine. You want to play it that way?"

"Oh, yes, I do. Ma'am." What was up with him? The way he called her "ma'am"?

It made her think of tangled sheets and his big hands all over her. "Have you gone insane?"

To that, he said nothing, just waited there with those arms she wanted wrapped around her crossed over his chest, his badge glinting aggressively in the hot afternoon sun as more than one car whizzed by not six feet away, the occupants watching wide-eyed through their side windows as they passed.

He still wasn't budging. She supposed she had to do something. "Fine. You want me out?"

"That's right. I want you out."

"Well, you got it, then. I'm getting out." She shoved open the door, swung her shoes to the gravel and jumped to her feet, grabbing the door as she did it, slamming it shut good and hard in her fury—and then wincing as she realized she'd probably startled her poor baby awake.

But no. Marybeth slept on.

And her husband had definitely lost his ever-loving mind. He stood silent and still as a statue. Beneath the wide brim of his hat, the lenses of his dark glasses reflected her own distorted image back at her.

She lit into him. "What is the matter with you? You can't just come after me in your cruiser. Seth Yancy, this is harassment, pure and simple. You should be ashamed of yourself."

Once again, he said nothing. But he did move at last.

He took off his hat and his sunglasses and set them carefully on the Tahoe's hood.

Only then did he speak. "It's not harassment, Jody." Now his voice was quiet. Tender, even. Really, what was going on here? None of this made sense. "I promise you it's not."

She glared at him sideways, totally lost as to what he was up to and also unwilling to back down. "Oh, yeah, well, if not harassment, what is it, then?"

What he said next almost buckled her knees. "This is me trying to find the way to tell you that I'm hopelessly in love with you."

She made a noise then. It wasn't a word, exactly. It was more a cry of pain and longing.

"Jody?" He looked suddenly terrified. "Jody, are you okay?"

She blinked at him owlishly. "Um. Yes. I think I am, yes."

"You sure?"

"Well, if I'm not I definitely could be. Now, where were you? Please, go on."

And right there, on the side of the road a little more than halfway between the Bar-Y and their hometown, Sheriff Seth Yancy dropped to his knees. "I love you, Jody." He stared up at her, and there was no mistaking the truth in his eyes. "Forgive me, Jody. Take me back. Make my life worth living. Please."

She gaped down at him. "I don't… What are you…? Seth." Her throat burned and her vision blurred with tears. "Oh, God. Seth."

"I've done what you asked for. And what you asked for was right. I talked to my father, and he made me see that we don't honor the dead if we refuse to be all we can be for the living. I love you, Jody. Let me give you my all. Let me be just for you—you and Marybeth and any other little ones that God might be willing to give us. Give me one more chance. You won't regret it. That is my promise. I swear that to you. That is my vow."

She blinked away the blinding wet heat of her tears and looked down at his upturned face, saw the truth in him, saw that somehow he had done it, put his guilt and his pain behind him enough to reach out for her at last. "You, um, ahem. Would you get up, please?" She offered her trembling hand.

He took it, strong fingers closing around hers, the wonder of his touch arrowing straight to her heart. "Jody." He swept upward. And he touched her face, a caress both reverent and full of tender care. His fingers brushed the curve of her cheek, and everything within her cried out in joy. "You are my love, Jody. You are my everything."

Another cry escaped her. She held out her arms.

That did it. He grabbed for her and yanked her close, wrapping her up in his heat and his strength and, at last, the miracle of his love. "One more chance…" He pressed his lips to her hair.

"Yes. Oh, yes. Oh, Seth. Thank God."

"I love you, Jody."

"And I love you."

And he lifted her chin and he kissed her, right there on the side of the road with several good citizens of Broomtail County rubbernecking the sight as they rolled by in their cars.

He kissed her and then he kissed her again. And then finally, when the baby woke up with a cranky little cry, he let her go and ushered her back into the Tahoe, opening the door for her, gently shutting it once she'd settled into the driver's seat.

He took his hat and sunglasses off the hood and then leaned in the window as she hooked up her seat belt and started the engine. "I'll follow you home."

"Yes." She glanced over her shoulder at her baby. Marybeth was quiet again, staring dreamily into space, her little fist stuffed in her mouth.

Seth said, "Keep to the speed limit, now."

"Yes, Sheriff. I will."

"I'm letting you off with a warning this one time. But I'll be keeping my eye on you."

"I will behave, Sheriff. I will be good."

"I intend to hold you to that."

"I expect nothing less," she replied. "And you'll see. I keep my promises. I will not disappoint you. We're going to have a great life together, you and me."

His stern mouth twitched at one corner. "Something tells me we're not just talking about speed limits here."

"Something tells you right. We're talking about everything."

"Now, there's a tall order."

"Everything, Seth. All that we have together, all that we are and all we will be. I love you, and it's everything to me that you can finally say you love me, too."

He leaned even closer. His mouth brushed hers. "I do love you," he whispered. "So much. With all my heart."

"See you at home," she whispered.

He straightened with a slow nod. "See you at home."

Epilogue

A year after Seth declared his love for his wife on the side of the road, Bill Yancy returned to live at the Bar-Y. A year after that, Jody was pregnant again.

In February of the following year, as a blizzard turned the world to white outside the ranch house windows, Jody had her baby right there at home without the aid of a single medical professional.

But Seth was with her through it all, the same as he'd been when she had Marybeth. More than once, he said how much he loved her as he fed her ice chips, rubbed her back and reminded her to breathe. She said she loved him, too.

But having a baby? If she'd only remembered how bad labor was, she'd have stopped with Marybeth. And when it came time to start pushing, she clutched his hand so hard the bones ground together, and she swore never in her life to have sex with him again.

Downstairs in the family room, Marybeth climbed into her beloved grandfather's lap. "Mommy sounds really mad, Pop-Pop."

Bill guided her head to rest on his shoulder and stroked her shining golden hair. "She's not mad, Bethie. She's just having a baby. She will be fine."

"You promise?"

"Oh, yes, I do."

"She sounds like she's crying, too, like she might have a bad owie."

"Could be. But she's a tough one, your mommy. And your little brother will be here before you know it."

Marybeth's half brother was born twenty minutes later. They named him Nicolas, after the uncle he would never get to meet.

Two years after that, Jody had a little girl, Darlene. And three years after that, another boy. They called him Patrick.

That same year, Josh Levinson, twenty years old and a sophomore at UCLA, asked to meet his birth mother. Jody and Seth welcomed him at the Bar-Y. Having grown up an only child, Josh was excited to discover he had four half siblings.

And at the age of forty-three, seven years after he married the mother of his brother's child, Seth Yancy remained sheriff of Broomtail County. He still had a flock of pretty admirers who showered him with baked goods and bright smiles.

Jody had no problem with any of those women.

She knew his heart belonged to her.

* * * * *

*Watch for book eight
in the unforgettable saga of*
THE BRAVOS OF JUSTICE CREEK.
*GARRETT BRAVO'S RUNAWAY BRIDE
is coming in October 2017,
only from Harlequin Special Edition.*

Things had certainly changed around here, he thought as he drove back to his house. Even Maude, who had once seemed as unchangeable as the mountains, had softened up a bit.

A veterans' group meeting. He didn't remember if there'd been one when he was in high school, but he supposed he wouldn't have been interested. His thoughts turned back to those years, and he realized he had some assessing to do.

"Come in?" he asked Ashley as they parked in his driveway.

She didn't hesitate, which relieved him. It meant he hadn't done something to disturb her today. Yet. "Sure," she said and climbed out.

His own exit took a little longer, and Ashley was waiting for him on the porch by the time he rolled up the ramp.

Nell took a quick dash in the yard, then followed eagerly into the house. The dog was good at fitting in her business when she had the chance.

"Stay for a while," he asked Ashley. "I can offer you a soft drink if you'd like."

She held up her latte cup. "Still plenty here."

He rolled into the kitchen and up to the table, where he placed the box holding his extra meal. He didn't go into the living room much. Getting on and off the sofa was a pain, hardly worth the effort most of the time. He supposed he could hang a bar in there like he had over his bed so he could pull himself up and over, but he hadn't felt particularly motivated yet.

But then, almost before he knew what he was doing, he tugged on Ashley's hand until she slid into his lap.

"If I'm outta line, tell me," he said gruffly. "No social skills, like I said."

He watched one corner of her mouth curve upward. "I don't usually like to be manhandled. However, this time I think I'll make an exception. What brought this on?"

"You have any idea how long it's been since I had an attractive woman in my lap?" With those words he felt almost as if he had stripped his psyche bare. Had he gone over some new kind of cliff?

Don't miss
CONARD COUNTY HOMECOMING
by Rachel Lee, available June 2017 wherever
Harlequin® Special Edition books and ebooks are sold.

www.Harlequin.com

Celebrate 20 Years of

Love Inspired®

Inspirational Romance to Warm Your Heart and Soul

Whether you love heart-pounding suspense, historically rich stories or contemporary heartfelt romances, Love Inspired® Books has it all!

Sign up for the Love Inspired newsletter at **www.Loveinspired.com** and connect with us to find your next great read from the **Love Inspired, Love Inspired Suspense** and **Love Inspired Historical** series.

THE WORLD IS BETTER WITH

Romance

Harlequin has everything from contemporary, passionate and heartwarming to suspenseful and inspirational stories.

Whatever your mood,
we have a romance just for you!